Silenced

Even in innocence, silence can come at a deadly cost...

Unfinished Business
Book 3

Juanita Kees

Silenced

Juanita Kees

Overwhelmed in the aftermath of her husband's death, Lily Bennetti navigates protecting her teenage son from his father's criminal legacy and the dangers that continue to stalk them. The secrets she keeps come at a high cost. If the detective on the case figures out the truth about her connection to a cold case murder, she stands to lose everything she has left.

When Mark Johnson delves deeper into his ongoing investigation of the murder of Tiny Watts, the last person he expects to be interviewing for it is a crime boss' widow. His gut tells him she knows more than she's letting on. Her bruises tell a different story. The way she defends her son suggests that the threat runs even deeper than her scars. He's determined to bring the notorious crime gang ruling the streets to justice, but at what cost?

About the Author

Finding hope in country towns with dark secrets ...

Juanita escapes the real world to create emotionally engaging stories steeped in crime, suspense, mystery and intrigue. Her books are set in dusty, rural outback Australia and on the NASCAR racetracks of America. Her small-town USA and Australian rural stories have made the Amazon bestseller and top 100 lists. Juanita also likes to dabble in the ponds of fantasy and paranormal with Greek gods brought to life in the 21st century.

Juanita graduated college with distinctions and a diploma in Proofreading, Editing and Publishing in 2011 and started her freelance writing business, Kees2Create Words. As a developmental and structural editor, she assists writers to polish their manuscripts for submission. In 2012, she achieved her dream of becoming a published author and now has multiple novels on the market.

When she's not working, writing, editing or proofreading, Juanita enjoys travelling to discover new worlds for inspiration. Mother to two handsome heroes and partner to a car enthusiast, Juanita also has a passion for fast cars and country living.

Juanita loves to talk books with readers and would love to connect. Contact her via:

Amazon Author:
https://www.amazon.com/author/juanitakees
Website:
https://juanitakees.com/contact/
Kees2Create Words Editing:
https://kees2createwords.com/
BookBub:
https://www.bookbub.com/authors/juanita-kees
Newsletter:
https://kees2createwords.substack.com/embed
Goodreads:
https://www.goodreads.com/author/show/6454477.Juanita_Kees
Book Love Book Club:
https://www.facebook.com/groups/607880523038543

Acknowledgments

A very special thanks goes to my friend James who was happy to spend hours on the phone with me, painstakingly answering all my questions about juveniles in detention and the legal process that takes place. Any errors in the legal context are mine and the situations in this story are purely a product of my imagination. James, you are a truly remarkable individual who believes in justice and who is dedicated to help young offenders change and grow.

Chapter One

Lily Bennetti's head swam. Red spots danced in her vision and an agonising throb beat at the top of her skull. She lifted a hand to touch the tender spot. Her fingers came away sticky with blood. Slowly, painfully, she lowered her hand to the cream, plush pile carpet. Her palm brushed across broken glass. The coffee table — she'd fallen when Gino had pushed her away, hit her head on it.

'You dumb arse piece of *shit*!' Gino's voice pierced her thoughts, dark and threatening, somehow scarier than the yelling she vaguely remembered from earlier. Luke's response was muffled. Through the haze of pain, she focused on the figures standing in front of her — one big and bulky, the other a mere featherweight.

Gino stood, feet apart and menacing as he anchored

Luke up against the far wall, his stance way meaner than the words he hissed through his teeth.

Luke gripped Gino's wrists in an effort to force his meaty hands from his neck. The terror in her son's body language sent fear barrelling through her. Bile rose in her throat. *Dear God.* Gino was going to kill Luke.

No. Lily stumbled to her feet. Blood rushed to her head, dizziness had her crashing to her knees. Desperation chased away the fear. She had to get to Luke. Her jaw ached where Gino had smacked her. She tasted the coppery tang of blood on her tongue where her teeth had sunk into the soft flesh of her lip. *No more.* She dragged her aching body up, using the sofa for support. As the little colour left in Luke's face drained away, Lily drew on all the strength she had left. Saving her son was all that mattered.

'*Stop*, Gino.' Desperation rang in her voice as she raised it over her husband's. Silence fell heavily on the lounge room. She staggered protectively toward Luke. Gino dropped his hands to his sides, fists clenched.

Lily gripped the torn sleeve of her son's shirt. Angry red welts criss-crossed the pale teenage flesh underneath. Then she saw it. The gun in Luke's hand pointed at his father's heart. 'Jesus, Luke. Don't do it. It's not worth it.'

'No, Mum. I'm done. Done taking his crap.' His voice was gritty. The purple marks at his throat evidence of the pressure his father had placed on his windpipe.

Lily placed a shaking hand over Luke's equally unsteady one. 'This isn't the way.'

Gino snorted. 'He doesn't have the guts for it, Liliana. He's weak. Takes after his mother. A no good, lazy sonofabitch. He doesn't have the spine to pull the trigger.'

Gino lunged forward to grip his son's wrist. It happened in slow motion, the way she'd seen it in movies. A shot rang out and surprise registered on Gino's face before his body crumpled to the floor with a bullet in his chest. Dark red blood seeped into the cream carpet as his life drained away. Silence stretched as Lily and Luke stood, the sound of the shot reverberating in their ears. The gun slipped from Luke's nerveless hands.

Detective Mark Johnson closed the notebook and turned it over in his hands, the words still clouding his mind.

GB came to work today, cornered me in the parking lot at M&M. I'm pissed off. I thought they'd leave me alone after the last bust. Someone's going to get hurt. I think it could be me. How did I get into this? I want out but I know they won't let me. I'm not scared to die. It's the other boys in the gang I'm worried about. Luke, Marty and Connor. Luke is too close. He and his mum are sporting shiners again. GB is getting crazier. I hate that he takes it out on his own family.

Cleverly concealed in the graffitied cover were clues that teenage gang leader, Tiny Watts, was murdered. All they had to do was prove it and find his killer. It should have been an open and shut case; a gang of troubled kids, a drug deal gone wrong. Instead, the more dirt he uncovered, the deeper the roots went.

Tiny had left a notebook of clues with keywords hidden in the bricks he'd drawn on the cover. Matching people to initials had created a jigsaw puzzle with too many missing pieces. At the same time, it connected the dots between three key players consistently. The initials SS, GB and NA appeared in almost every sketch, disguised by graffiti or imbedded in objects.

Having read a chunk of the notebook Tiny had left in his room at the shelter, Mark was convinced that GB was Gino Bennetti. The prominent gangland lawyer certainly didn't have a squeaky-clean record. But how was he involved? Who was he protecting? The video evidence they'd gathered from the convention centre parking garage proved his car was there at the time Tiny disappeared. But there was no proof he'd snatched the boy.

'Hey, Buddy, put your toys away.' Mark's partner, Harold Jones, stuck his head around the door. 'We've got ourselves a murder in interview room one.'

Mark shoved the notebook into the evidence bag. 'They're bloody dropping like flies.' Tired, he lowered his feet off the desk and straightened. The last few months had exhausted him. Trouble had struck way too close to home for his liking. His sister's daughter was kidnapped and held for ransom by her stepfather, Paul Price. Paul had owed money to Gino Bennetti. The link between her kidnapping and Tiny's gang had grown stronger with each piece of new evidence that came to light and he didn't like the path it was taking.

'Boy aged seventeen. Neighbours heard shouting, like a fight. Loads of thumping. They heard the woman crying, shouting at them to stop. A shot, a scream and ... nothing. Neighbour called it in. She was too scared to go over there.' Harold dropped the manila file on his desk. 'It looks like the boy killed his father.'

Mark flicked through the scribbled case notes, his eyes coming to rest on the victim's name. 'Fuck!'

'That's what I thought you'd say.'

'I guess that takes Gino Bennetti off our list of suspects to interview in the Watts murder. Tell me more.'

Harold shrugged. 'The boy's not talking. They're both pretty messed up.'

'They?' Mark frowned at Harold as he closed the file and stood.

'His mum's in there with him. Boy's name is Luke. He's one of the Tag Raiders.'

Tiredness fled and Mark's back stiffened. 'The boy

named Luke — the boy Tiny mentioned in his notes — is Gino Bennetti's *son*?'

'They don't call you fuckin' super sleuth for nothin', do they?' Harold mocked.

'The lines are becoming very blurred, Harold.' Mark waved the file at the door. 'Let's go talk to the kid.'

As he walked through the door of interview room one, his gaze fell on Gino Bennetti's widow. Lily Bennetti looked like a bedraggled angel who'd been to Hell and back on a bumpy ride. Long, honey-blonde hair lay tangled around her shoulders. Even streaked with blood from the cut on her left cheek, it shone like a halo under the hot, industrial lighting. She turned to face him, and his breath hitched in his throat. Watery blue eyes blazed red from under swollen lids, a dark bruise bloomed on her right cheek and her top lip swelled around a split in the middle.

Anger churned in his gut. If the man wasn't already dead, he'd fucking kill him himself. No-one deserved to take a beating like this. He turned his gaze to the boy, watched him flinch as he pulled out a chair and it scraped against the concrete floor. Mark noticed the scars on his arms first, exposed by the ripped sleeves of his shirt, and made a mental note. Drugs, self-harm or abuse? Luke's hands trembled on the table, bloodied and bruised, knuckles swollen and split. He'd given Gino a good bashing, but by the look of his left cheek and eye, he'd been dealt a few nasty blows too.

Mark sat in the chair and faced them. Lily Bennetti looked nothing at all like the photos he'd seen in Gino Bennetti's file. Gone was the confident, smiling young woman on the arm of her good-looking Italian husband. In her place was a broken doll, her silky pale skin a patchwork of angry welts and bruises, her shoulders hunched as she hugged her arms tightly against her stomach. He ignored the tug at his heart, the urge to comfort her, to tell her it would be alright.

'Mrs Bennetti, I'm Detective Mark Johnson,' he began. 'Do you have any objection to me asking your son a few questions?' Lily shook her head but didn't look up, so he tried again. 'I'm sorry, but you have to answer the question for the record.' He tried to keep his voice neutral, but gentleness crept in as her eyelids flickered.

The pain it caused her to speak was obvious. This time she raised her eyes to his. 'No.' She winced as she touched her lip below the split.

'Thank you.' He wanted to reach out to touch her hand reassuringly, but she'd clenched them tightly in her lap. He turned to the boy. 'Luke, would you like to tell me what happened?'

Silence met his question and the boy continued to stare at his hands. Mark sighed. It was going to be like pulling teeth. Lily unclenched her hands and laid one over Luke's with a squeeze. He pulled away with a jerk and sunk deeper into his seat.

'It's okay, tell him.' She withdrew her hands and clenched them in her lap.

Luke's jaw flexed as he fought his inner battle. Mark watched. Body language was a dead giveaway. What this boy would say came from deep beyond the physical injuries.

With a sigh, Luke sat up in his chair. He kept his eyes on the table, but he unclenched his hands as he began to speak. 'Dad and I got into a fight. He called me a dumb arse piece of shit.'

'Why were you arguing?'

'I told him I was done. I didn't want to work for him anymore. He got mad.'

'Done with what?'

'Running his deliveries.'

Mark made a note. Gino Bennetti was a criminal lawyer. What deliveries could his son possibly do for him? A question for later, he thought as it raised a red flag in his gut. 'What happened then?'

'He grabbed me by the throat and pushed me up against the wall. Mum tried to stop him.'

Mark's gaze flicked to Lily's hands as she twisted them nervously. His eyes on her face, he asked Luke, 'What did your dad do then?'

Luke looked at his mother for a long moment, his eyes glittering with tears he struggled to hold back. 'He punched her in the face, and she fell backwards onto the coffee table. He knocked her unconscious! He could have killed her. I'm not sorry the bastard's dead.'

'*Luke.*' Lily's voice broke over his name.

'It's true, Mum!' He raised his voice and his mother flinched. 'He treated us like shit! Made us do stuff that —'

'What did he make you do?' Mark encouraged when Luke's words ended abruptly. If the boy clammed up now, it could be a while before they drew the truth out of him. Experience had taught him to strike while the adrenalin was high. 'Luke, we're here to help you. What work did you do for him?'

Luke paused and looked at his mother for a long moment. Silence spread in the interview room like a dark and gloomy cloud. At Lily's nod, he continued, 'I delivered parcels for him. I didn't want to do it anymore, not after Tiny Watts ... died.'

Mark straightened in his seat and narrowed his eyes at the hesitation in the boy's voice. 'So, you and Tiny Watts were friends?'

'We were in the same gang. The Tag Raiders.'

'What was in the parcels you delivered for your father?'

As Luke took a breath to continue, the door to the interview room flew open and banged against the wall. 'Shut up, you idiot. Detective Johnson, my client will not be answering any further questions.'

Mark was on his feet immediately. The man reeked of slimy, no-good lawyering. His expensive suit and shoes, gold watch, dark looks and meaty fists screamed *underworld* as he thumped his Armani briefcase on the table next to Luke. Luke and Lily stood and backed away. Fear flashed across their faces. Lily gripped Luke's upper arm, her knuckles white.

'No!' She squared her shoulders, her spine ramrod straight, fear in her eyes, determination in her voice. 'No.'

'Yes!' He turned to Mark. 'I'm Gino's business partner from Albero and Bennetti lawyers. Nic Albero. I'd say it was a pleasure, but I'd be lying. Is my client under arrest?'

'He's not your client.' Lily's quiet voice shook.

'Don't be a fool, Liliana!' The big man took a step toward them. 'The boy is *not* in a position to argue. Neither are you.' He flashed them a warning look that fell just short of mean.

Harold stepped forward from where he'd stood, quietly observing the interruption. 'Since there would appear to be a conflict of interest here, the court will assign a lawyer for Luke if you prefer, Mrs Bennetti.'

'Conflict of interest?' Albero's outrage echoed off the concrete walls. He moved surprisingly fast for such a bulky man as he spun toward Mark and Harold.

Harold stepped between Albero and Lily, pushing him away a couple of steps. 'As the victim's business partner, I doubt the boy would get a fair defence. This is a murder case, Mr Albero, and you have too much to gain if the boy is found guilty.'

'That's bullshit and you know it,' Albero sneered.

'Come to think of it, how did you know we had him in custody?' Mark asked.

Albero hesitated, his eyes shifting to the wall. 'It's on the news.'

Mark stepped forward, arms across the expanse of his chest. 'There's an embargo on the press releasing any details on the shooting because the suspect is under age. Try again.'

He'd spent enough years on the force to recognise Albero's type, even if the lawyer's reputation didn't speak for itself. Bugging phones, tracing calls and intercepting police data were all part and parcel of his defence tactics.

'*I'm* his lawyer!' Albero ignored the underlying accusation.

'No!' said Lily. This time her voice was strong and confident. 'Luke will have a court lawyer.' She pushed Luke behind her and stepped around Harold. 'We don't need your ... services, Nic.'

'You're making a *big* mistake.'

'Get out.' Her shaking hands belied the deadly calm of her voice.

Albero's eyes narrowed on hers. 'You'll regret this, Liliana.' He turned and walked away. The door slammed behind his departing bulk with the force of a gunshot and Lily Bennetti, tired, battered and broken, crumpled to the concrete floor.

Lily awoke to the clinical white walls of the hospital emergency department, the beep of equipment and the echo of footsteps in a corridor. Confused, she lay a moment trying to get her bearings. Her heart pounded to life as she remembered — Nic Albero.

'Luke!' she cried and struggled to sit up. God, her ribs ached, and her head pounded in rhythm with her heart. The needle in her hand twisted painfully and she looked around to see it attached to a drip.

A gentle hand touched her arm and she jerked away. Wincing, she turned her head to see Detective Mark Johnson straddling a chair next to her. Arms folded along the backrest, chin resting on muscular forearms, his short, dark blond hair was messy, and he looked ... tired. Deep grey eyes studied her from under brows a shade darker than his hair, his gaze intense. Lily felt she should be intimidated by it, yet somehow it was reassuring, comforting.

'You and Luke are in hospital. When you fainted, Luke got a little upset. The doctor says you might have concussion.'

'Where's Luke?' she asked, her voice fringed with panic.

Big, tanned arms unfolded, and he waved a long-fingered hand at the curtains around the next cubicle. 'He's on the other side of those. They've got him under sedation. It's okay, Mrs Bennetti, you're both safe.'

She fell back against the pillows and closed her eyes. 'Safe? I don't think you understand, Detective.'

'Help me understand. Why are you so terrified of Nic Albero?'

'Nic isn't one to take no for an answer.'

'He threatened you.'

'Yes.' Her fingers tightened on the bed sheets. 'I defied him. Broke the family code. Nic is ... was ... Gino's cousin.'

Now he'd be out for blood. They were as good as dead. They knew too much and with Gino gone and no-one to keep them in check, Nic knew they were an even bigger risk to his operation. She turned to look at the man sitting in the chair. It would be so good to share her burden with someone she could trust. For a long time, she'd suspected her husband was involved in the underworld of drug trafficking and crime. What she hadn't expected was that he'd drag their son there with him.

'Why don't you want him to defend your son?'

'Because I don't trust him.'

If Luke went to prison for murder — even detention

in juvie while he waited for his case to be heard —
Albero's thugs would get to him, and he'd be dead in
weeks. They were sitting ducks. There was nowhere to
run. She closed her eyes as tears squeezed from beneath
her lids and ran down her cheeks.

'Mrs Bennetti ... Lily ... if there's something you
know about Nic Albero, you need to tell me. If you want
a fair trial for your son, you can't keep information to
yourself.'

'I can't ...' Luke wouldn't get a fair trial at all if the
police found out he was in the car when Tiny was
murdered. He was a witness, an accessory. The evidence
would send him to prison for good. 'I can't.'

'You have my word. We will make sure you and
your son are safe during this investigation.' The deep,
soothing voice did nothing to calm her nerves.

'What use is your word, Detective? It's no
protection against a car bomb, or a fire or a bullet...or
worse.' Her bruised cheek ached with each word, her lip
bled with the effort to speak.

Albero would be determined to get rid of any
witnesses to Tiny's murder, especially when he'd been
the one to hold the boy down while his partner, Serena
Snow, administered the deadly overdose that killed his
runner. Her husband had held Luke and forced him to
watch, promising he'd be next if he didn't do as he was
told.

'My handbag ... where is it?' she asked suddenly, her heart in her throat.

He pulled it out of the cabinet next to her bed and held it up. 'In here. I thought you might need it for identification.'

Oh God. Had he looked inside? Had he found the notebook? It was all there, recorded in Luke's diary along with dates and times of every delivery he'd done for his father, and the people who'd received them. All coded neatly so the untrained eye wouldn't see the subliminal messages, except for the moment when Tiny Watts was murdered. Her head pounded with pain as she tried to concentrate. If he found it and had it decoded —

His eyes narrowed on her face but all he said was, 'While you and Luke are here, you have round-the-clock guard. Depending on the autopsy findings and the judge's decision at the preliminary hearing, Luke could be placed in remand at the detention centre. We're expecting the autopsy results in by the end of the week.'

Lily drew in a shuddering breath. 'Remand? How well will he be protected from ... the other inmates?'

'That depends on the level of danger he's in. Lily, if there is some reason you feel you or Luke are in danger, tell me please.'

'And where will he be until the hearing?' Her voice cracked and her eyes stung with unshed tears.

'When you're feeling up to it, I'll take your statement and we can get this under way. Once I have your statements, I'll submit the evidence. A lawyer from the district attorney's office is on his way now so he can be present when I interview Luke. He'll try to arrange a preliminary hearing via video link as soon as possible. We won't know where Luke will be placed until then.' The quiet reassurance in his voice did nothing to settle the nausea that rolled in her stomach.

'I need to see Luke.' She pushed the thin covering of the blanket away and pushed up off the pillows.

'Stay there, I'll open the curtain.' Mark stood and walked around the bed to sweep the curtain aside.

Lily turned her aching body toward the bed next to hers. Luke lay sleeping, curled up in foetal position, his bruises dark purple against his pale skin. The steady beep of his heart through the monitor and his gentle snoring reassured Lily he was still alive. She settled against the pillows, a sigh shuddering through her. Keeping him alive would be her next challenge.

'I'll give you my statement, Detective.' Lily's voice was faint but determined.

Mark sat and pulled his mobile phone from his pocket. 'Do you mind if we record the interview with this?' He held it up and wiggled it between long, strong fingers. 'It's much easier than taking notes and more reliable in case I miss something.'

Lily eyed him cautiously, her gaze taking in the strong contours of his face. The straight eyebrows and forehead — now marred by a frown — assured her he was a solid thinker who would consider all the facts first before passing judgement. She'd learned to read facial expressions and body language over the years ... she'd had to with Gino. Without them, she would have a lot more scars. She'd learned when to steer clear of confrontation. God knows, it could have been her or Luke lying downstairs on a cold slab in the morgue if she hadn't learned when to back down. Still, could she trust this man who had the power to take everything they had left away from them?

'Whatever it takes.' She was so tired of running from the truth.

'Tell me what happened today.'

Lily sighed heavily. 'Gino's punch knocked me down. I fell and hit my head on the coffee table. It must have knocked me out for a bit.' Absently, she touched the tender spot near the top of her skull and felt a raw knot the size of a small egg.

'Your skin was split. They've glued the cut. How long do you think you were out for?'

'Not long. When I came around, Gino and Luke were fighting.' She shivered as she relived the scene in her head. Gino with his hands around Luke's neck...Luke's strength no match for anger. 'Luke couldn't breathe. I could see him turning blue from the force of Gino's hands around his neck. I tried to stop him and that's when I saw what Luke had in his hand. I don't know where he got it from.' She clutched the cold cotton of the hospital blanket like a lifeline thrown from a boat. The tears she'd held back trickled down her cheeks.

'Got what from?'

'The gun. Luke had a gun in his hand. It must be Gino's. I tried to stop them fighting, got between them. Gino made a grab for the gun, and it went off.' Her breath hitched and she closed her eyes. 'He fell.'

'So did Luke shoot Gino?' Mark's voice was soft, encouraging.

'No ... I don't know ... I ...' She swiped at the tears on her cheeks. 'All three of us had our hands on the gun, Detective. When Gino grabbed Luke's hand, it went off.'

'Do you think Luke would shoot his father deliberately?'

Lily looked to where her hands gripped the sheet, knuckles white, shaking. If she said yes, she would incriminate him. She hesitated and looked at Mark, seeing nothing but a detective looking for answers, his face open and honest. Still the words hesitated on her tongue.

He met her gaze with empathy in his own. 'That wasn't a leading question, Lily. I'm trying to establish his state of mind. The two of you suffered trauma prior to the shooting. It makes a difference.'

Lily hesitated a moment longer. Her instinct said to trust him and that's all she had left. 'No. I think he was trying to scare Gino into backing off. You have no idea the torment he put us through.'

'Tell me,' Mark said.

As Lily opened her mouth to speak, Luke's voice whispered across the space between their beds. 'Mum.'

Lily sat up and swung her legs over the side of the bed. Dizziness hit her like a brick wall, and she sank back.

'Easy,' Mark warned, a hand at her waist for support as he pulled her drip stand closer.

She flinched away, the recoil automatic. Without a word she stood, slower this time. Using the drip stand for support, she walked the short distance to her son's side.

'I'm here, Luke.'

'You okay, Mum?'

'Yes, I'm okay. We're okay.'

'I'm sorry.'

Lily looked at her son, lying against the stark white pillows. Dark bruises and dried blood marred his otherwise flawlessly pale skin. His sharp cheekbones hollow in the harsh hospital lighting. He was a shadow of the happy little boy she'd once bounced on her knee and cuddled close at bedtime.

'It was an accident, Luke.' She pressed a kiss against his temple.

'But I *wanted* to kill him. Is it so bad to want to kill him after what he did to us?'

Lily ran a hand through his hair and stroked his forehead. 'He can't hurt us anymore, baby.'

'What will happen to us now?'

Lily looked at the detective, who stood silently at her side. His eyes met hers, empty of judgement and full of reassurance. 'We tell the truth and rebuild our lives ... one brick at a time.' *And pray to God we stay alive long enough to live it.*

Chapter Two

An hour later, Luke's lawyer arrived, and they gave their statements to Mark. It was only when the questions came to Nic Albero that both Luke and Lily held back. Mark watched their reactions with interest as they dodged the subject in an attempt to draw his attention away from the dubious activities of one of Perth's most influential lawyers.

There was no doubt in his mind that Nic Albero was a threat. He noted the tremble of Lily's hands at the mention of his name and Luke's gaze that shifted to his mother's before he'd answer, giving careful thought to his words.

Mark made a note to do a little more checking on Albero. 'Thank you,' he said, pushing the button on his phone to end the voice recording. 'I have what I need.'

'What happens now?' Lily's voice was raw as she reached for Luke's hand.

In all the time he'd been on the force, Mark thought he'd never been so undecided on what to do with a suspect. Right now, that's all the boy was. A suspect. Yes, he'd held the gun that killed his father, but it didn't mean he'd pulled the trigger. Fingerprinting would determine that.

His conscience nagged against arresting Luke. A prison cell was not the place for a child and juvenile detention wasn't much better. In fact, sometimes it was worse, especially where drugs were involved. Surely they'd suffered enough for one day. With them being held for observation overnight, it would give him time to go away and process the evidence.

'Detective Johnson, could I have a word with you outside?'

The lawyer excused himself and walked out of the ward and into the corridor. Mark followed, his curiosity piqued by the unusual request as he pulled the door closed behind him. Giles Pritchard had represented many an accused in Mark's arrests. They'd known each other a long time. For him to request a private word could only mean he had concerns about the Bennettis too.

'Off the record, Mark, I'm sure you know Bennetti wasn't exactly a straight arrow. I have no doubt you'll do your homework on that. His partner, Nic Albero, is no saint either. I'm probably not telling you anything you don't already know, right?'

'I'm onto it.'

Giles nodded. 'That's what I thought. Albero won't be happy his kingpin is dead. He'll be looking for retribution. Personally, I don't think either of them is safe. I'm going to do my best to keep the boy out of juvenile detention while we wait for his trial. These days it can take anything up to eighteen months or more for a case to be heard. Neither he nor his mother will last that long.'

'They may be a little broken, but I don't think they're as fragile as they look.'

'That's not what I'm talking about, and you know it. It's not their state of mind I'm worried about, it's their safety.'

'I have to enforce the law. He had a gun, and *that* gun killed a man.' Mark's voice rose and echoed in the corridor, torn between compassion and duty.

A nurse passing by held a finger to her lips and uttered a stern, 'Shh!'

Giles sighed and patted Mark on the shoulder. 'Down, Tiger. I'm not negotiating his innocence yet. I'm asking you not to place him in detention until you have all the facts. Take my word for it, the boy's not a threat to anyone else. I've arranged the preliminary hearing for tomorrow morning at 9:00 a.m. assuming you're placing him under arrest.'

Mark rubbed a tired hand across his face. 'I'm debating it. I'm a bit reluctant to lay any charges yet given the circumstances. At this stage I could take him in for involuntary manslaughter, which may be upgraded depending on the evidence against him.' Charging a kid for murder? Perhaps he was getting too jaded for this game.

Giles smiled. 'It's the best you can do right now. So, since they'll be in for observation until the hearing tomorrow morning, you'll leave them under guard?'

Mark nodded. 'I wouldn't want my witness or accused compromised in any way.'

'That's what I thought. Now I have a little suggestion to make. If I can convince the judge, we could get Luke into the Tiny Watts Teenage Rehabilitation Centre with TJ and Scott Devin until his case goes to trial.'

The knot of tension in Mark's neck eased a little. 'Yes, that would work. The centre is building a good reputation with their program, and their success rate in rehabilitating juveniles is growing. It makes sense to keep two out of three of the Tag Raiders out of trouble with young Marty already a resident up there. And, of course, having them together will make the investigation into Tiny's murder a little easier to handle.'

Giles winked. 'Exactly. The boys will talk, compare notes. They might feel more confident supporting the evidence you've already garnered.' Looking very pleased with himself, Giles patted his briefcase. 'Now, I have work to do setting this up for tomorrow.'

Judge Julia Carmody's stern face appeared on the screen set up in Lily and Luke's private room.

'Present your case, Mr Pritchard,' she said, her tone curt.

'Thank you, Your Honour. Luke Bennetti is charged with involuntary manslaughter.'

'I've read the case, get to the point.'

'Your Honour, I don't believe Luke Bennetti is a flight risk or a threat to the general public. This offence took place under extreme circumstances as you can see from the physical trauma Luke and his mother have suffered.'

'The boy had a gun, Mr Pritchard. He pointed it at his father, knowing it was loaded and ready to fire. I'd call that a conscious act.'

'I'd call it self-defence, Your Honour.'

'Semantics. I'm not here to play word games.' Judge Carmody turned her attention to Luke. 'Mr Bennetti, you realise the severity of your actions, I trust?'

'Yes, Your Honour.' Luke's voice shook as he replied.

'Fortunately for you, I can see that you and your mother *have* suffered extensive injuries during this incident. Give me a reason why I shouldn't send you straight to juvenile detention.'

Luke hesitated and looked at Lily for assurance.

'Tell her, Luke.'

'Because ...' His voice broke around the word. He swallowed hard and tried again. 'Because I was protecting my mother. He punched her and pushed her into a coffee table and then he tried to strangle me. I had to stop him or we'd both be dead!'

'That's no excuse for killing a man.'

'Your Honour —' Giles intervened.

'Wait your turn, Mr Pritchard! Give me something to work with, Mr Bennetti.'

Luke sat a little straighter in his chair and clutched Lily's hand tightly in his. 'This wasn't the first time my father laid into us. My mum has put herself in the way of his fists too many times to stop him hitting me. I didn't mean to shoot him. I didn't even know the gun was loaded. I just wanted him to *stop*.'

'Where did you get the gun?'

'From my father's holster when he turned from me to hit my mum. He always wore a gun under his jacket.'

'Mr Pritchard, what are you asking for?' Judge Carmody tossed her reading glasses onto her desk.

'To release him on bail until his trial, Your Honour.'

She folded her hands on top of the case file. 'And how do you propose to keep him out of trouble until then?'

'Scott and TJ Devin have set up a teenage rehabilitation refuge here in Perth. It provides a stable home environment and activities to keep teenagers off the streets.'

'The Tiny Watts Teenage Rehabilitation Centre. I've heard of it.'

'They will ensure Luke meets his bail conditions. There is also the option of him signing up for the apprentice program they run out of their dealership. A student counsellor visits the apprentices on a weekly basis to mentor them. They now have four qualified mechanics on staff who graduated from the program. None of them have reoffended.' He paused to give her a moment to process the information. 'Detectives Johnson and Jones are weekend volunteers there, as are other emergency services personnel.'

'Mr Bennetti, what are your thoughts on that?'

'Uh ... yes.' He looked at his mum and then at Giles. 'Yes,' he said, louder this time. 'I'll sign up for the program.'

'Fine. Bail is set at $2500. You will report to the detectives once a week and enrol in the apprenticeship program, during which time you will remain in residence at the rehabilitation centre under the care of Scott and TJ Devin. I want to see weekly reports from you on his progress, Detective Johnson and Mr Pritchard. All behavioural reports will be taken into consideration when it comes to Mr Bennetti's trial and sentencing.'

'Yes, Your Honour,' replied Mark, his hand resting gently on Lily's shoulder.

'Let's wrap this up then,' said the judge. 'The court order will be delivered to your offices today, Mr Pritchard. Mr Bennetti, from now on, it's your responsibility to meet your bail conditions. I don't want to see you again until your trial. Stay out of trouble.'

'Yes, Judge Carmody. I will.'

'Be sure that you do.'

The screen went blank, and silence hung in the air a moment.

Lily's shoulder trembled under Mark's hand, and he squeezed it reassuringly. She turned teary blue eyes to his and covered his hand with hers. He tried to ignore the zing that travelled through him at the contact.

'Thank you,' she whispered.

Unable to speak around the lump in his throat, he nodded. He was a cop, for God's sake! But there was something about Lily Bennetti that made him want more than to serve and protect at the level his duty required. Right now, with her looking at him like he was some kind of hero, he wanted to scoop her up, take her home and promise no harm would ever come to her or Luke again.

She dropped her hand from his and turned to the lawyer. 'And thank you, Mr Pritchard.'

'It's not over yet unfortunately. We still have a lot of work to do before the sentencing. But for now, you and Luke need to rest. I believe TJ and Scott are on their way to introduce themselves. I didn't see any point in wasting time, so I contacted them last night,' said Giles.

'You must have been pretty sure of the outcome,' replied Lily.

Giles shrugged. 'Either way, I would have gotten them involved. They're a great couple who do a great job.'

'And there's someone up there you know already, Luke,' added Mark. 'Your friend Marty is staying with them at the moment.'

Luke nodded and for the first time since he'd been brought into custody, the boy smiled a little.

Lily wiped at the tears on her cheeks. Mark handed her a tissue, their fingers brushing as she took it. His body tingled at the light touch. He took a step away from her and as he looked around the stark white room, he vowed to keep a cool head. He had to remain objective. As pretty and fragile as Lily Bennetti was, he had no right to feel even the slightest attraction for her.

With his focus off Lily for the first time since he'd brought her in to the hospital, he looked around the shared room they'd put them in. The emptiness of it struck him, the lack of flowers or get well soon cards. Where were her friends, her family? Were Gino and

Luke all she had? He made a mental note to look into her background.

'Is there anyone I can call for you, Lily? A friend, family?' he asked, his curiosity piqued.

Lily shook her head. 'No, thank you. There's no one.'

Those few words told him all he needed to know, along with the sadness in her eyes, the emptiness of her tone. Lily Bennetti had no one to turn to. The kind of man Gino Bennetti was would have hand-picked her friends if he allowed her any at all, alienated any family she might have had, and isolated her from the world. He'd seen it too often before, studied cases where women were held in captivity, and not even the closest neighbours knew it.

He allowed himself to feel anger toward the man responsible for the position she was in and worse, the condition he'd left her in. It was up to him to bring that same man's killer to justice, a boy defending his mother while fighting for his own life. Sometimes, his job sucked ... big time.

'Well then,' said Giles, interrupting his thoughts, 'I'd best be on my way. I'm sure you two will want to get out of here as quickly as possible and get Luke settled. TJ and Scott shouldn't be too much longer.'

'I'll walk you to your car, Giles. Harold and I have a few questions for you about another case I'm working on. Lily, we'll be back in a moment. Will you and Luke be okay alone for a while?'

'Of course,' answered Lily. 'The doctor should be in soon to discharge us anyway.'

Lily battened down the sense of unease as the doctor went through the motions of examining them for discharge and writing up their charts. Soon they'd be free to go. She knew *where* to but not to *what* — a stranger's home for Luke and an unknown future for both of them.

The door opened and Lily turned, expecting to see Scott and TJ Devin. Instead, Nic Albero strutted confidently into the room. Her blood turned to ice. Surely he wouldn't do anything here.

'Liliana, I'll take you and the boy home. I'll sign the discharge papers since I'm your next of kin.' His voice brooked no argument as he gripped her arm, his fingers digging cruelly into her soft flesh.

Lily tried to tug away but he held firm. 'We'll order a taxi, thank you.'

Mean eyes narrowed on his face. 'It was an order, not a request.' He leaned down to whisper in her ear. 'The less you resist, the easier I'll make it for you.'

'Mr Albero, Luke and his mother will need to spend some time with his case worker. They won't be leaving just yet. Luke is now a ward of the court, so your signature on the discharge papers would be null and void.'

Lily sagged with relief at the sound of Mark's voice from the doorway.

'I can wait for Liliana. I am a patient man.'

'I have no doubt about that. Mrs Bennetti and her son will be escorted home after the meeting. I'm sure you have clients to attend to?' Mark placed a hand at Lily's waist and steered her away from the big man. Albero was forced to release her from his grip.

'I'll be waiting, Liliana.'

She shivered, but the warmth of Mark's hand was reassuring. 'Stay away from us, Nic.'

With one last angry glance, Albero walked out.

'What was that about?'

'Nothing,' answered Lily as she looked around to see where Luke was. He stood to one side close behind Harold Jones and she breathed a sigh of relief.

'Lily, you're as white as a sheet. He scares you.'

She felt the burden of their secret weighing heavily on her shoulders. How was she going to keep Luke safe? The apprenticeship program would make him an open target in public. She nibbled on what was left of her nails and dismissed the thought of asking Mark for help. If she did, she'd have to tell him the whole story.

Mark placed a hand over hers and pulled gently until

she stopped worrying her thumbnail. 'Out with it,' he said.

She looked into grey eyes that had seen into the darkest corners of her life and knew she couldn't lie. He'd know. If she told him the truth, he'd be forced to follow up and go after Albero. Where would that put Luke?

With a sigh, she shook her head. 'It's nothing. Nic is a little scary, that's all.'

His look said he didn't believe her. 'I won't push, Lily, but if there is something you're not telling me ...' Those stormy grey eyes bored into her soul. '... I will find out.'

Lily dropped her gaze first and focused on the strong hand that swallowed hers in its grip. 'I know.'

'Then tell me.'

This time when her eyes met his, they glistened with unshed tears. *If only I could.* 'I can't.'

'Excuse me, Mrs Bennetti? May I come in?'

Lily turned away from Mark's searching gaze to face the woman who poked her head around the door. The pretty, petite blonde took a step inside.

'My name is TJ Devin, and this is my husband, Scott.'

'Please, call me Lily.'

'Lily.' TJ smiled as she handed Lily a bouquet of gerberas. 'We're from the Tiny Watts Teenage

Rehabilitation Centre. Scott and I run the apprenticeship program at M&M Motors.'

'It's a pleasure to meet you,' said Lily, accepting the flowers. She touched the soft, silky petals gently. Pink, orange, red and yellow swam together in a rainbow of colour as she blinked to clear the sudden tears. 'Thank you ... no one's ever given me flowers before.' Gino refused to have them in the house. Dying flowers made a mess. Not that he'd ever had to clean it up. He'd always had someone to clean up after him and it seemed nothing had changed even in death.

A big, warm hand patted her shoulder gently and she raised her eyes to Scott Devin's. In them, she saw warmth and understanding. 'You and my mum will get along well then. She has enough roses to give away to stock a flower market. You'll never be without flowers again.'

TJ laughed. 'Not just with roses, either. Luke will start work with us on Monday. Are you okay for him to move up to the centre accommodation today?' TJ asked.

Lily's uncertainty hovered. How safe would he be from Albero up at the centre and at work? Asking the question would only raise suspicion. It had all sounded good at first, but now the doubts nagged at her thoughts. She felt the touch of Mark's hand on her shoulder and turned.

'He'll be fine, Lily. The boys from the workshop look out for each other,' he said.

How did he do that? How did he always seem to know what she was thinking? Was she that transparent? She'd be best off guarding her emotions from now on.

'Thank you. Yes, it's fine for him to move up to the centre today. I'll ... need to pack some of his things.'

She dreaded going back to the house. Had someone cleaned up the mess? Were the investigators finished there? Would she be allowed inside? How would she feel walking into the house where her husband died?

'I'll give you a lift home,' Mark said. 'Luke could go on ahead with TJ and Scott. I'm sure Marty is looking forward to having company.'

Fear knotted in her throat. Could she let Luke go with these strangers? 'Luke?'

'It's fine, Mum. It'll be cool to hang out with Marty 'til you get there.'

'If you're sure —'

'I'm sure.'

Luke hugged her close for a moment and she relished it. He seldom breeched the gap these days, growing more and more distant as he'd been dragged into the underworld, powerless to fight against it. Now Gino was gone. Lily tried to feel regret and failed. She'd stopped loving him long before the abuse had started. To Gino, she was simply a wife, a necessity to complement his social standing. He'd saved all his affection for his long line of mistresses.

'Well, then if you wouldn't mind, Detective?' she said.

As much as she hated to admit it, Lily was thankful for the escort home. Albero's threats weighed heavily in her mind, but it was time to stand on her own feet. Gino was dead. She was free. Free from the pain of a marriage gone wrong. Free from the violence and lies. Now all she needed was to be free of Albero. There were only two ways to achieve that — run or hide. Hiding forever wasn't an option. That wasn't freedom.

Over the years she'd mourned the loss of hopes and dreams, of wasted years and the crime that had turned Gino into a monster. Perhaps that monster had always been there, waiting to be awakened. Lily ignored the shaft of pain that lanced her chest. Even in death, Gino's power reigned over them.

She felt the sharp nudge of feelings of worthlessness and inferiority creeping in. How often had Gino reminded her of her weaknesses? She wasn't pretty enough, smart enough, well-dressed enough to attend his fancy functions unless it suited him to have her there. She would never be able to hold a conversation with intelligent people because she was a loser, a failure, inept in a crowd. Her cooking skills weren't good enough, so they'd had to hire a cook. The way she dressed wasn't to his liking, so he chose all her clothes and then gave her little opportunity or occasion to wear them. Birthdays, holidays, Christmases were all about the great Gino Bennetti. Everything had to be his way.

In the early days, when Luke was little, she'd argued with him over it until it became too painful to go against his wishes. So, they ate what he wanted to eat, went where he wanted to go, did what he wanted to do until they no longer did anything together at all. Now it was time to move on.

'Mum?' Luke's voice interrupted her thoughts. 'Let's go.'

Lily shook off her morbid thoughts, straightened her spine and took a step toward the door. What would be, would be and they'd deal with it one step at a time.

What was Lily Bennetti hiding? Mark watched her face for a moment before pulling away from the curb. He was glad she'd agreed to let him take her home. It showed she trusted him, even if only a little. That pleased him more than it should, and not for professional reasons either. He forced his thoughts away from how easy it would be to like this troubled angel.

Despite using his best interrogation tactics during questioning, the shutters on her thoughts remained tightly closed on certain areas of their life with Gino Bennetti. It wasn't hard to identify the signs. She'd given them only what they needed to know about her husband's murder. He was convinced she knew more.

Watching her was no hardship. Lily was a beautiful woman whose character had taken as much of a beating as her body had. Soft-spoken and gentle-natured, like a kitten that needed a home, she'd touched a part of Mark's heart he preferred to keep for himself.

He flicked the indicator switch and turned left onto the road that led to the affluent Perth suburb of Brampton Park. Silence stretched between them. He left her to her thoughts while he processed his own. How would she feel when she opened the door to the house? Pretty crap, he'd imagine. It was a good thing he was there. Returning to the crime scene now, he would get a different perspective of it. He could study it objectively, see things he might have missed the first time around, all while Lily packed up Luke's stuff. How would she feel staying alone in the mansion? Would she be afraid? He wasn't convinced she'd be safe.

'Forensics has finished in the house and the clean-up crew have gone too. Will you be okay alone there?' He voiced his thoughts out loud.

Lily turned from staring out the side window at the passing scenery. 'I ... I think so.'

The hesitation in her voice had Mark's gut twisting. She was trying so hard to be brave, yet he could feel fear radiating off her in waves. 'Is there somewhere else you can stay? Family? Friends?'

She shook her head. 'I'll be fine.' Her fingers twisted in her lap. 'I'll put on the alarm, or maybe stay in the guest house out the back.'

'Do you think Albero will be a problem, Lily? Is he likely to cause trouble?'

She shrugged. 'I don't know. I really hope not.'

The quiver in her tone told him otherwise. She was scared ... dead scared. He wouldn't be surprised at all if Albero showed up at the house later, once he was sure she was alone. The question was what did he want with Lily? His behaviour at the hospital was suspicious, if not more than a little threatening. It might pay to put a patrol car on the street tonight, Mark thought as he pulled up in the driveway of the mansion.

'Call me if you feel uncomfortable at any time and I'll make arrangements for you,' he said. It was his duty, wasn't it, to serve and protect his witness? He had two dead bodies on his case files, and both were connected to the Bennettis and Albero.

Lily looked out the window at the house and shook her head. 'I need to stand on my own two feet. Now is a good time to start.'

'You've been through a lot in the last twenty-four hours, Lily.' He switched off the engine and turned in his seat.

'No more than I have in the last sixteen years. It's Luke who matters now. Will he be safe up at the centre?'

'That much I can guarantee. TJ and Scott run a tight ship. There is supervision up there at all times. Scott's parents, Rose and Bill, are only too happy to play the role of surrogate grandparents to the kids and Sarge, the Rottweiler, does a pretty good job of playing guard dog ... when he's not licking people to death.'

Lily smiled and Mark's heart skipped a beat. He could only imagine the power her smile would pack when her face healed.

'He always wanted a dog,' she said.

The wistfulness of her tone had him reaching for her. 'You'll get through this, and so will Luke.'

'What if the court finds him guilty and he goes to prison? There were drugs involved. The inmates will either make him a target or he'll be forced into the gangs. Sometimes it's worse inside the prison system than out.'

'I'll do everything in my power to help, but you have to be honest with me all the way.' He patted her hand, so small and white against his tanned skin. 'Are you afraid of Nic Albero?'

'Yes,' she whispered.

'Why?'

He moved his hand to her arm. Was she feeling the connection too? He wanted ... no, needed her to trust him, to believe he would protect her and her son while they searched for the truth. Mark could almost hear the gears turning in her head as she churned her dilemma over in her thoughts. Yes, the lovely Lily Bennetti was definitely hiding something.

'Nic was involved as deeply as Gino was in money laundering and drug smuggling. They used innocent kids as runners. Kids like Tiny Watts. Luke and Tiny were mates. I'm afraid that ... Nic thinks Luke knows more than he does. Nic Albero will stop at nothing to get what he wants. Nobody dares stand in his way.'

The anger in her tone faded as panic rolled over it. She shifted in her seat and picked at the hem of her skirt with fingers that bore the cuts and broken nails to prove she had a reason to be frightened. He watched her face, noting that she didn't look at him. Her eyes flickered to the left. Not quite the truth, then. Was she protecting Luke or Albero? No, they were clearly scared of the man. It had to be Luke.

'Lily, I know you're not telling me the whole truth. I understand you have concerns for Luke. I won't push you for answers right now but know this ... you can trust me when you're ready to tell the whole story. I won't let anything happen to you or Luke, that's a promise. Not a cop's promise, but mine.'

'I trusted once and here I am, the widow of a drug dealer.'

Her chin quivered and he reached out his free hand to cup it gently. He turned her face toward him and looked deep into her eyes. He felt the impact of the desperation he saw there. It twisted and churned through him until it tugged at his heart.

'Will you at least tell me if Albero causes you any more trouble?'

She held his gaze for a long moment until desperation turned to hope. 'Yes.'

'Then go inside, get Luke's things and we'll take this one step at a time.'

She nodded. 'Thank you.'

He let go of her chin while he still could. The temptation to pull her into his arms was strong and he cursed the timing again. Getting out of the car, he stepped around the hood to open the door and help her out. She stood close to him and took a deep breath as she looked up at the three-storey building.

'Would you like me to come inside with you?' His gaze followed hers. The elaborate Tuscan style house sprawled across a double-sized block of land and towered over the neighbouring houses. Imposing, with wrought iron bars covering the windows, Mark thought it reminded him of a prison, one that had since seen murder and was no stranger to violence. It would always house the ghost of the man who'd ruled it. What other secrets did it hide?

'Please.' The word whispered out as she released her breath on a nervous sigh.

He held out his hand for the key, taking note of the video surveillance cameras overlooking the front door and down the front path. Gino Bennetti had certainly had a thing about high security.

She slipped it out of her pocket and handed it over. 'Thanks.'

'You're welcome,' he said, brushing a finger across her cheek to wipe away a tear. 'Let's go.'

He held her hand and led her up the path to the front door. Bloody Fort Knox, he thought as he inserted the key into the lock on the heavy front door. The weight of it suggested reinforcement of some kind. To keep his family in or to keep his enemies out? Pushing it open, they stepped over the threshold onto cold, white marble tiles. No warmth, no homeliness filled the vast, almost clinical entrance hall. Where was the personality, the woman's touch he'd expect from a woman like Lily? His gaze caught on the hall table where shards of coloured glass scattered the wooden surface and fell to the hideous Murano sculptures that now lay smashed on the floor. Mark looked around at the damage. Someone had trashed the house looking for something. What hadn't been torn to shreds was smashed or slashed. The nauseating smell of gas drifted toward them and instinct kicked in. Mark grabbed Lily's hand.

'Run!'

An explosion from the kitchen in the rear rocked the mansion and it shuddered around them. Flames stretched through the doorway. Without hesitation, Mark swept Lily into his arms and ran as windows exploded behind them. As he sprinted across the road, he heard the crash of bricks as the rear wing of the house crumbled under the weight of the roof, showering them in a cloud of grey ash and mortar. Lily shivered against his chest as shock set in.

'You okay?'

'Yes.' She clung to his shoulders and buried her head against the comfort of his neck. 'No.'

He held her tightly, taking in the smell of her hair and the sweet perfume she wore. His heart pounded against his chest in time with hers.

'Jesus!' he muttered against her hair. 'That was close.'

Lily said nothing as she burrowed deeper for a moment before pushing at his chest.

'Put me down ... please.'

With one last hug, he lowered her to the pavement where she collapsed on the grass and stared at the blaze that now engulfed what was left of the mansion.

Lily let out a breath, shaking, afraid to move. When would this nightmare be over? She jumped as her phone vibrated. Albero's number came up. She ignored it as Mark dialled emergency services on his phone, listening to the comfort of his voice directing them to the site. He hung up and dialled again.

'Harold, get to the Bennetti place as fast as you can. There's been an incident ... a gas explosion.' He snapped his phone shut and put it in his pocket before dropping onto the grass next to her. 'Lily, I'm offering you and Luke witness protection in exchange for your testimony against Albero and anyone else working with Gino.'

Lily shivered but remained silent. No amount of protection in the world could save them from Albero's wrath.

Sirens blared as emergency vehicles rounded the corner into the street and came to a halt. A flurry of activity materialised around them as firemen charged their hoses and police ran yellow tape around the area to cordon it off. Crowd control officers urged bystanders to stay away as they poured onto the street for a sticky beak.

Lily took a deep breath as Mark moved closer and put an arm around her shoulders. She leaned into the warmth and comfort he offered.

'What the hell happened? Now will you tell me what it is you're hiding, Lily? Someone was in your house. They trashed the place and turned on the gas.'

And destroyed any evidence that might prove Luke innocent, she thought. Her phone vibrated in her hand. She looked at the screen. *Call 321, you have one new message.* Ice spread through her veins and tears stung her eyes. Albero wouldn't give up until they were dead. With a shaking finger, she dialled in to her message bank.

'*You're making it hard for yourself, Liliana. There's nowhere to run. You were lucky the detective got you out in time. I'll make sure you don't get that chance again. You're nothing but a pain in my arse right now.'* Impatience rang in Albero's recorded voice message.

Her teeth worried her lower lip as she hung up. She looked around, trying to spot him in the crowd. The roar of a familiar engine reached her ears as his black sedan rounded the corner and disappeared. He was right. There was nowhere to run, no-one she could trust, unless ...

Mark's hand rested gently on her shoulder. 'What's going on? And make it the truth this time.'

Lily refused to meet his eyes as fear nudged shock aside. She couldn't. He'd see too much. Fight or flight? The instinct to run and hide burned in her mind. Did she and Luke have the strength to keep running?

'Mark?'

A voice called out and Lily sagged with relief at the interruption. Maybe Mark wouldn't have time to press for answers. She couldn't reveal their secret, she wouldn't subject her son to the torture of prison. The alternatives weren't looking promising either.

Without taking his eyes off her, Mark called, 'All clear...Lily, what more can I do to earn your trust?'

Lily kept her eyes on his booted feet and remained silent as Harold approached with a paramedic. Mark stood and helped Lily to her feet.

'I'm going to leave you with the paramedics while I fill Harold in,' he said. 'Will you be okay?'

Lily nodded as the paramedic placed a medical kit next to her. 'I'll be fine.'

Mark released her hand, and she missed the warmth and reassurance of it immediately. As she watched him walk away with Harold, she wished with all her heart she could trust him, that her nightmare would end, and she and Luke could be free.

Wrapped in a thermal blanket, Lily looked on as the paramedic cleaned the cuts and grazes on her arms and legs. She cooperated as he listened to her chest and lungs, looking for signs of smoke inhalation, her movements mechanical. Across the road, fire-fighters battled to save what was left of her home from the monstrous flames. A struggle that failed when the walls crashed to the ground and sent embers sizzling upwards into the steady stream of water pouring from their hoses. There was no going back now.

'I can't leave you alone for five minutes without you getting into trouble,' said Harold as he walked beside his partner.

'Not the sort of trouble I was looking for,' Mark replied. He stopped walking and looked at Harold. 'I think we have another attempted murder on our hands.'

'You *think*?' Harold stood beside him and flicked at

the ash on his shoulder. 'I thought maybe you just like getting dirty.'

'Something like that.' His partner knew him too well. Fifteen years as a team did that. 'I think our widow is hiding something. My gut is telling me it has something to do with Tiny Watts.'

Harold shrugged. 'Your gut's been right before. You've been studying his notes. Besides the gang connection, did Tiny mention anything else in his notebook about Luke Bennetti?'

'Not much. He seemed to hang out more with Marty.'

'He's the one staying up at the refuge with Scott and TJ, right?'

'Yep.' Mark rubbed the nape of his neck tiredly. 'I might go and study the notes some more after I've dropped Lily off at TJ's. Want to come around for a beer?'

'Nah, I'm going to get some sleep after I clear up the mess you've made here. You're the super-sleuth. I'm just your sidekick. Catch ya later.'

Mark grinned. 'Lazy fat cat. Go on then, go and get your beauty sleep. God knows you need it.'

Harold punched his shoulder. 'We can't all be pretty boys. You reckon that Albero bloke will give the widow any more trouble? Can't say I like him much.'

'At least we agree on one thing. Someone went to a

lot of trouble searching the Bennetti house before blowing it up. I wonder what they were looking for.'

Harold shrugged. 'Whatever it was they couldn't have found it. Why else would they blow up the house?'

'Here's the weird bit. Right after the explosion, Lily's phone rang. It struck the fear of God into her, and I suspect it was Albero. He knew she and Luke were heading home today and when.'

'You think he might have something to do with the explosion and was ringing in to see if she survived.'

Harold had the knack of turning Mark's questions into statements. 'I'm thinking he's in way deeper than we think and I doubt it's on the right side of the law.' Mark sighed as he waved a hand at where Lily's house lay in a pile of smoking rubble. 'I think we have enough evidence to support putting them in witness protection. I've made the offer.'

'We have to find that missing link. I thought Bennetti was the kingpin in the drug operation but now I'm wondering if he was just the brawn.' Harold frowned and scratched his head.

'I think you may be right, and I believe our answers lie in the drawings and notes Tiny Watts left behind. That's why I want to go through them again.' He hitched his keys from his pocket and handed them to Harold. 'You take my car, I'll take yours and I'll see you in the morning.'

Harold looked across the road at where Mark's car

stood parked in Lily's driveway, now a battered wreck under the rubble of what used to be the garage. 'Thanks for parking it under cover for me.' He swapped keys with Mark. 'The boss is going to be pissed at you! Bring coffee. That crap they have in the office is worse than donkey pee.'

Mark chuckled as he walked away and dialled TJ's number. Harold may be as rough as guts, but he had a heart of gold.

TJ picked up. 'Hello?'

'Hey, TJ. Mark here. Have you got room for one more? There's been a little accident at the Bennetti home.'

'Oh my God, Mark! Was anyone hurt?'

'Only the house. We got out in time.'

'Shit! What happened?'

'A little trouble with a gas leak. I'll fill you in when I bring Lily up.'

TJ sighed. 'As long as you're both okay. I'll open one of the cabins up for Lily and Luke. I'm guessing it will be long term?'

'It's looking that way. You're a gem, TJ.'

'You're welcome,' she said and hung up.

Reaching Lily, he placed a gentle hand on her shoulder where she now sat inside the doors at the rear of the ambulance.

'They finished patching you up?'

'Yes.'

'I've spoken to TJ. She's offered you one of the cabins at the refuge for as long as you need it.'

'Thank you.'

She had no choice but to accept, he mused. Where else could she go? 'I'll drive you up there now. We need to talk.'

Lily nodded. He held out a hand to help her down as he watched the expressions flit across her face. Sadness, defeat and hopelessness tugged her mouth. Exhaustion added to the grey of her face. She swayed and leaned into his touch.

Mark realised he was in trouble as he watched tears form on her grubby cheeks. The sight of them hurt. The thought of what had brought her to this point seared his gut. Right now, he didn't want to ponder on why he felt that way. All he was prepared to acknowledge was that falling for Lily Bennetti right now would be a big mistake. The feel of her body against his, the rightness of it and this godforsaken *need* to protect her placed him way out of his league. Yet he couldn't deny her the comfort, nor could he deny himself the pleasure of giving it.

His arm slipped around her shoulders to hug her close for a brief moment before guiding her away from the ruins of her life.

Chapter Three

ark didn't push Lily for answers as they drove up the hill to Karalee. He'd give her the time she needed to process the events of the day. The sinking afternoon sun shone through the window, bathing her in its golden glow. Her bruises bloomed and the cut on her cheek would leave a small scar. Lily Bennetti was still a battered angel.

Perhaps the destruction of her house was a good thing. He suspected that without the force of Gino Bennetti's mean personality, Lily would blossom once again. There was no argument, she was one tough lady. What was in the house that had prompted someone to ransack it and blow it to Hell? Had they destroyed evidence that might prove Luke innocent? Or were they after something else? Lily and Luke were in danger, of that he was certain but unless she accepted his offer of witness protection...

'Think about my offer, Lily.'

She straightened in her seat as they pulled up the driveway of the refuge, her white-knuckled hands in her lap the only indication of her distress. Mark pulled the car into the clearing that served as parking and cut the engine. He placed a hand over her clenched fists.

'Trust me, Lily. I'll do everything I can to help you and Luke.'

'I know.' She sighed as she met his searching look. 'But that doesn't make it any easier.'

The defeat in Lily's voice tugged at his heart. She met his gaze bravely, yet he read uncertainty, mistrust and deep sadness in eyes the colour of blue violets. He imagined how they could sparkle with laughter, with the happiness she deserved. His gaze dropped to her lips. He wanted to see those soft, full lips widen in a smile and hear her laughter. What did her laugh sound like? Her lips parted as she drew in a breath, and he wondered how she'd taste.

'Mum!'

Luke's voice broke the spell. Mark dragged his gaze away from temptation as the passenger door of the car was thrown open and Luke peered in. His eyes were immediately drawn to the fresh scrapes and sooty clothes.

'What happened, Mum?'

'The house ... it's gone.' Lily choked back fresh tears. 'There was a fire ... gas explosion.'

Terror lit in Luke's eyes as he glanced Mark's way. He looked at Lily and said, 'It will never be over, will it?'

'No, Luke, it won't. Not unless ...'

Luke held her gaze as a silent message passed between them, the air thick with tension. Mark opened his door and got out. Luke retreated, pushed his hands deep in his pockets and walked away to stand next to Marty. It seemed his gut feeling was spot on again. There was no doubt in his mind now that it was Luke she was protecting. He just needed to find out why. Reaching the passenger side of the car, he held out a hand to help Lily out.

'Thank you,' she said.

His chest brushed against her shoulder as he closed the door. The heat he felt every time he saw or touched her, rushed through him. It had to stop. She was a victim, a new widow, *a case* for God's sake. He had no business being attracted to her, at least not until they'd settled this case. If nothing else, he had to solve this case and he would do nothing to compromise the outcome. That included becoming personally involved with the family of the victim. Even when they were victims themselves.

The door slammed a little harder than necessary.

With a hand on her arm, he guided her to where Scott and TJ waited with the boys.

'Nice to see you again, mate,' said Scott, shaking Mark's hand then turning to Lily.

'Welcome to the refuge. Marty, Luke and I were about to go and toss a football down near the creek. Want to join in, Mark?' He waved a hand to where Luke and Marty had already set off to the clearing, talking animatedly.

Mark shrugged. 'Sure, why not?' He might get a chance to talk to Luke. From the rigid set of the boy's shoulders, he could tell whatever young Luke and Marty were discussing, it wasn't football.

'Come, Lily.' TJ stepped forward to take her hand. 'We'll watch the boys from the veranda and enjoy a glass of wine. I think this situation calls for at least one glass. Red or white?'

Mark watched as TJ led her away. At the top of the stairs, Lily turned and looked at him. With a tilt of her head, she smiled. He felt the impact of that smile all the way to the toes of his size fourteen feet.

Tranquillity surrounded her, as Lily sipped her glass of chilled Margaret River wine. The classic dry white and TJ's laid-back company made it easy to relax, despite the horror of the day. That coupled with the sound of

Marty and Luke's chatter blending with the deeper male voices, had her letting down her guard a little. God bless these people — these strangers.

She welcomed the distraction as a Band-Aid on the events of the day. How long had it been since she'd heard Luke laugh? Her son had become a stranger to her, retreating further into his shell the older he got. Occasionally, she saw a glimpse of the happy boy he'd once been. Until his father had drawn him into the hellhole of drugs and murder. He'd robbed Luke of his childhood and now his involvement in the underworld trade had taken their home too.

Losing the house didn't matter. It was a prison, a reminder of years they'd spent at the mercy of a man who'd become a monster. They'd escaped with their lives ... just. It was time for them to start living again. Here in the peaceful surroundings of the Perth hills, she could almost see a future for them. Almost.

Lily shook off the gloomy thoughts and turned to TJ who sat relaxed in a chair with her feet up on the veranda rail. 'Thank you for having us here at such short notice.'

TJ smiled as she looked down at the creek where the boys challenged the men in a game of touch football. 'No problem at all. Marty will be happy for the company and Scott gets on really well with the boys. He'll make a great dad one day. Soon hopefully.' She turned her head and grinned at Lily. 'We're still enjoying the practice.'

Lily grinned back. TJ's smile was infectious. 'How did you and Scott meet?'

'Ah, now there's a story. More wine?'

Lily nodded and held out her glass. 'A good story, I hope.' Golden liquid filled the glass. 'Thanks.'

'You're welcome. It could have been a sad story. Scott fired me on his first day at M&M.'

'No!'

TJ laughed. 'Oh yes, for breaking the safety rules and wearing stilettos in the workshop. My choice of shoes wasn't intentional. You see, my car had broken down on the way to work and I had to walk a little way to M&M to organise a tow.' She sighed. 'Luckily though, he saw his mistake, apologised and the rest is history. We've had our hiccups though, like the time his ex-girlfriend showed up during the Apprentice Awards Ceremony. What a piece of work that bitch is — Snow by name and cold by nature.'

Snow. The name echoed in Lily's mind, drowning out the rest of TJ's words as the wine curdled the contents of her stomach. *Please God, no.* 'Snow?' She forced the question from vocal cords strangled with dismay.

'Yeah.' TJ wrinkled her nose. 'Serena Snow. She tried to frame Scott for laundering dirty drug money. It made the papers on the east coast and caused a bit of a scandal, so he came west. Boy am I glad he did! I fell in love with him when he came with me to find Marty who'd played hooky from work. I'm glad he came along. We found Marty at the gang clubhouse. He'd overdosed on a mixture of LSD and Ice.'

Lily's heart hitched as dread trawled through her. *Oh my God!* She was afraid to ask, but she had to. 'Was it only Marty there?'

TJ shook her head. 'Young Tiny Watts was with him. He was the supplier. We think there were two others there too, but they'd disappeared by the time we got there. Scott was great. I don't know what I would have done without him. He held Marty while I tried to keep him calm until the ambulance arrived. I've seen kids under the influence of drug cocktails before, but that was the worst reaction to one I've experienced since working with these kids.'

So, Luke *was* there that day. It explained why he'd come home pale and scared. Lily shivered. LSD and Ice, the drugs that killed Tiny Watts while Luke was forced to watch. She swirled the wine in her glass and wished she could flush away the awful memories it held for her son. The revelation that Serena Snow was somehow connected to Scott Devin scared her even more. How safe were they really?

TJ reached across to pat her hand. 'Lily, we know Luke is one of the Tag Raiders. There's a fourth boy, Connor. He's the youngest and most vulnerable. Scott and I will do everything we can to help these boys stay safe and out of trouble.'

'I'm his mother. I could have put a stop to it long ago, but I didn't even try.'

'None of this is your fault. Look in the mirror and see beyond the bruises. You did what you thought was best, for your safety and Luke's.'

Lily wondered if TJ would still feel the same when she found out it was Gino who was behind the supply of the drugs she fought so hard to protect Marty from. 'Yes, I did but it cost a child his life.'

With a sigh, TJ relaxed in her chair and took a sip of her wine. 'There was nothing you or anyone could have done to stop that. Scott is always telling me I can't save them all, but I'm damned if I'll stop trying. We can only do our best from now on, together. That's what creating this centre was about — saving the kids one at a time. You've got us on your side now, Lily. Here comes Mark. If you're not ready to trust us yet, there's the man you can.'

She watched as Mark made his way up the grassy slope toward them, a satisfied smile stretching his lips, dimpling his cheeks. Lily felt something quiver inside her. It was hard to ignore his presence. Strength and reliability emanated from him, all wrapped up in golden good looks made all the more attractive by his lack of ego.

'He's a nice package, isn't he? All that solid muscle

and good looks mixed with a killer personality,' sighed TJ. 'It's just as well I adore Scott, otherwise I might be tempted.'

Lily smiled. There wasn't much she could say to that other than agree. Watching him walk confidently toward them settled her fears a little. TJ was right. She had to learn to trust him. He'd pulled her from her burning house, stood with her when it collapsed and now he held their future in his hands. She had to start somewhere. Why not with Mark Johnson, a man who'd shown integrity and had stood up to Nic Albero?

He'd rolled up the sleeves of his white shirt to reveal strong, corded forearms, pumped from tossing the football. His tie was stuffed carelessly in his pants pocket and the top three buttons of his shirt were undone to reveal a smooth, solid chest. That killer smile alone would have women on their knees.

Attraction stirred and swirled within her. She shifted in her seat at the tingling sensations pooling in places untouched for too long, shocked she was feeling anything at all. Hero-worship, it had to be. It couldn't be anything else.

With a will of their own, her eyes followed the line of his buttons to the belt at his waist and she watched slim hips move with a rhythm that had heat surging through her. Her hand shook a little with the force of it, sloshing the wine over the side of the glass.

TJ laughed. 'Let me take your glass, Lily. If that look in his eye is anything to go by, I'd say he wants a word with you.' She lifted the glass from Lily's nervous fingers and placed it on the table between them. 'I'll take drinks down to the boys. Come on over when you're done.'

Lily's voice couldn't make its way past the dryness in her throat, so she nodded instead. She wanted to beg TJ to stay. Alone with Mark, he'd ask those questions she knew she couldn't ignore. He stepped up onto the veranda and Lily's breath hitched as his eyes searched hers. There it was again, that lightning strike that surged between them. The feeling he could see the secrets and lies in her heart. What would happen if she told him the truth?

Silence stretched as TJ handed him an ice-cold beer before bounding down the stairs. He sat in the chair she'd vacated and drank, long and deep. He settled down with a contented sigh.

Lily's gaze followed the movement as he stretched out long legs and crossed them at the ankles. She clenched her hands in her skirt and wondered what it would be like to climb into his lap atop those muscular thighs and bury herself against the comforting warmth of his chest. The thought was far too tempting after years of a cruel, cold, painful and loveless marriage.

'Why did you stay with him, Lily?'

Mark's intuitive question unsettled her. He could

read her thoughts far too easily. What chance did she have of keeping her secret?

'For Luke's sake. I thought if he saw his son grow up, he might be more of a loving father. I hoped he might change, soften a little.' Restless now, she stood and walked to the edge of the veranda. 'Naïve and young, that's what I really was. He'd never change, and I did Luke more harm than good by staying. I blame myself. For not leaving him sooner, for not standing up to him, for letting him steal Luke's innocence. I'd give anything to go back in time and change things.'

Near the creek, Luke played a handball and whooped as Marty caught it and ducked out of TJ's reach. Guilt sank heavily in her stomach. By staying, she'd put him in danger and destroyed them both emotionally. She'd denied him a happier childhood.

'You can't blame yourself, Lily. Gino was a bully, a manipulator who used his own family for gain.'

'Yes, but I'm Luke's mother, and I let it happen. Luke was such a happy child, always laughing, picking flowers for me on the way home from school. Then he hit those awful teenage years when they're so vulnerable and easily misled, so determined to grow up, to find themself, to fit in with the crowd. I never thought for a moment Luke would get involved with drugs and gangs. Nor did I think it would be his father who got him there.'

Lily heard the soft rustle as Mark sat up in the chair.

She looked back to see his hands clasped around the beer bottle, watching the condensation drip onto his long fingers. A frown drew his eyebrows together as he processed her words.

People in happy, balanced relationships couldn't understand the chains of domestic violence that bound partners in intimidating relationships. They never saw the darker side of drug and alcohol abuse — the mood swings, the anger or the brutality it brought when turning a sound mind insane. Mark would have seen the damage it could do. He'd understand.

'Did Gino ever try to get counselling?'

'He would've had to admit to having a problem first. Gino came from a long line of abusive husbands. I wish I'd known that at nineteen.' She turned to face him now, her back against the veranda railing.

He looked up from peeling the label away from the bottle. 'What do you know about a woman named Serena Snow?'

Why did that name haunt her at every turn? What did she know about the silver-haired bombshell, other than that she was a cold, murderous bitch ... and what she'd read in Luke's diary? She'd appeared from the east coast out of the blue. Lily shivered at the revelation that she was connected to Scott Devin. Gino certainly hadn't talked about her. He'd kept his business very private. The reasons for that were obvious now as his death raised more questions. On the rare occasions he'd discussed business with his wife it was only to brag about his successes. The failures never warranted discussion, only pain.

'Only what I know from the media. I rarely attended the law firm functions.'

'I don't think he knew her through the law firm, love, unless he'd defended her at some stage.' Mark stood and walked over to stand next to her. He placed his hands on the veranda rail and looked across at where TJ and Scott chatted to the boys. 'Tiny Watts kept a diary. In it, he recorded dates and initials — which we suspect are drug deliveries — along with some interesting drawings we think might be clues. Do you know if Luke did the same?'

Grey eyes pinned hers and Lily froze. *Dear God.* She dropped her gaze from his to look out over his shoulder at the bushland. Luke's diary had the power to send her son straight to prison, to destroy his life for good. It would lay bare his soul and reveal everything she'd tried to protect him against. She lifted her eyes to his and felt the force of a look that dared her to lie as he continued.

'Gangs have a way of keeping records in such a way that they need interpretation. Graffiti, sketches, coded messages in tattoos, even their language is riddled with code words.' He reached out and touched her arm gently, his skin warm against the iciness of hers. 'I want to help you ... and Luke, but I need your help in return.

We have reason to believe Tiny Watts was murdered and that your husband and Serena Snow were involved somehow. Help us find the missing pieces of this puzzle, Lily.'

Lily leaned against the railing away from the comfort of his touch, her back stiff. He didn't know the half of it. How much longer could they hide from the truth anyway? She wanted to trust this man. She liked his easy manner, the caring he showed, but that wouldn't help Luke behind bars and at the mercy of other prisoners.

Mark took a step forward, his hand outstretched, palm up. 'Let me help you, Lily. If there is something — any evidence at all — that will take these monsters off the street, I need to know.'

'I can't! You don't understand ...'

'I want to understand what it is that has you so afraid. I want to see you and Luke live normal, happy lives again. I want you to tell me the truth.'

He stood almost toe to toe with her now. She felt the warmth of his body, the temptation to sink into the comfort it provided. Her body swayed toward him with the strength of the pull. Strong, warm fingers tipped up her chin gently. Dark grey eyes searched hers for the truth and promised a safe haven from harm.

'My offer of witness protection is still on the table. Take it and let's end this nightmare of yours.'

Lily hesitated a moment longer, torn between telling

the truth and protecting her son who had suffered so much at the hands of these criminals already. She'd borne this burden alone for too long. The strength to fight against it waned as the ache of her strained muscles surfaced.

'Yes, he has a diary.'

With a sigh, Mark pulled her into his arms and held her against the beat of his heart. Lily listened to the comforting tattoo for a moment, savoured the warmth of his arms and allowed herself to believe he meant what he said.

What on earth had possessed him to take her in his arms? Her breasts pressed against him, her ear to the erratic thumping of his heart and the crown of honey-gold hair within kissing distance. Throwing caution to the wind, he kissed the top of her head. She stiffened against him but didn't move away. Perhaps she should have. While his instincts screamed for him to step away, his hands stroked her back with a soothing rhythm and he felt her relax against him.

For a moment longer he held her, until his body stirred with need. Gently, he dropped his arms from around her and stepped away from temptation. Neither of them was ready to act on the attraction that buzzed between them. Neither of them would be until the truth no longer kept them apart and Lily's inner scars had healed.

'The others are making their way back.' He sighed, not sure whether to feel relieved or annoyed. 'Can we talk later? After you and Luke have settled in?'

Lily nodded. 'Sure.'

'Mum, would it be okay if I stayed at the main house with Marty tonight?' Luke was out of breath as he reached the stairs. His normally pale skin was flushed from the exercise and the long fringe that usually hid his face was tucked out of the way behind his ear. 'Mum?'

Mark knew the instant Luke became aware of the tension in the air. Fear replaced the excitement on his face, and he cast a quick look in Mark's direction.

'Yes, that's fine, Luke. If it's okay with TJ,' said Lily. Her reassuring nod had the teenager's shoulders relaxing again.

'Fine by me.' TJ stepped onto the veranda. 'Are you going to stay for a barbeque, Mark?'

'Thanks, TJ.' It looked like he wasn't going to get back to the station to retrieve Tiny's diary tonight. A pity, he thought. It would be good to compare the two diaries for similarities in events. Providing of course, Lily consented to showing him Luke's version. At least staying for dinner wouldn't give her time for second thoughts.

'Good, you can help Scott carry the supplies over to Lily's cabin. The ladies at the second-hand shop dropped off a donation of clothing we can go through later, Lily. I'm sure we can find something in there to tide you over until we go shopping.'

He watched her walk inside with TJ and wondered what it would be like to kiss her. He'd been so tempted earlier with the warmth of her in his arms. Yet seeing how scared she was, he couldn't afford those thoughts. Not yet. Not until the case was closed, Lily was stronger and whatever secret she was hiding no longer lay between them.

Mark turned to see Luke watching him with wary eyes. His fringe covered his eyes again and a flush of excitement replaced Luke's sullen expression. Should he try to talk to the boy? Even as he took a step forward, Luke backed away.

'Hey, Marty. Why don't you and Luke go fire up the barbeque out back. It needs a bit of a scrub,' Scott ordered the boys.

'Sure can, Scott,' replied Marty. 'Let's go, mate.'

As the boys walked off, Scott turned to Mark. 'Don't rush him. Let him settle a bit. Trust will take a while.'

'Yeah, I know.' Mark sighed. 'Did you see much of Luke before Tiny's death?'

'No. He was too young for the apprenticeship program. He slipped through our fingers. Bennetti made sure of it.'

'Did you know about Serena Snow's connection

with Bennetti and Albero during your relationship with her?'

Scott's ex-girlfriend was a nasty piece of work with even nastier connections. Mark wasn't surprised to find she was also involved with drug trafficking. Blackmail, money laundering and falsifying contracts was another skill she'd added to her crime resume in the ongoing case against her. All they needed to do was to catch her.

Scott shook his head. 'Serena introduced them as old friends. She brought them to the Dealership to buy a fleet of delivery vans. I remember wondering what lawyers would want with delivery vans but didn't question the sale. In hindsight ...'

Mark patted his shoulder. 'Hindsight, pity it always comes too late.'

The scandal had rocked the media for months when Serena Snow had slapped a harassment suit on her former partner, Scott Devin. But it had gone far deeper than a failed relationship as they'd begun to find evidence of fraud intending to set Scott up as a scapegoat for laundering drug money.

'Do you think Albero was behind the explosion at the house?'

Mark nodded. 'He's been ringing Lily, threatening her. Harold pulled the phone records.'

'What do you think she's hiding?'

'It's more about who she's protecting.'

'What happens if she's withholding evidence?'

Mark ran a hand over his face and rubbed at the day's growth of beard. 'It could get ugly for both of them.'

'I guess we need to make sure it doesn't.'

'We're going to try our hardest,' Mark agreed.

'*Oi,*' called TJ from the veranda. Both men turned to see her with a pile of linen in her arms. She tossed it neatly into Scott's. 'Why don't you boys go and make up the beds in Cabin One while we get the salads ready.'

'And here I thought we could sit, watch footy and drink beer while the kids did the barbeque,' grumbled Scott.

'Not if you want to sleep in a bed tonight.' TJ turned and went inside.

With a shrug, they set off toward the row of four cabins further up the slope behind the house. Razed during a fire six months earlier, the community had pulled together to help Scott and TJ rebuild the refuge accommodation. Now they stood guard over the garden they'd dedicated to Tiny Watts, the ruins of the chimney where he'd hidden his letter to TJ stood proudly in the middle.

Scott whistled for his Rottweiler, Sarge, who followed happily behind them. 'On guard,' he told the dog. Sarge turned toward the view of the driveway and flopped down with his head resting on his gigantic paws. 'I'll leave him outside the door of the cabin tonight. He'll keep an eye on her so she's not alone.'

'Can he use a gun?' Mark laughed.

'No, but he's been sharpening his teeth on Marty's cricket stumps. Chewed the damn things in half.'

Lily watched the two men from the kitchen window and thought about Luke's diary. She'd burn it herself if it didn't also hold evidence that would take the drug ring down. Now Mark knew about the diary, dare they use it to cut a deal for Luke?

Thank God she carried it with her in her handbag or it would have been lost with everything else today. Or worse ... what if it had gotten into the wrong hands? Albero — or his thugs — were looking for something. There was no other reason for the mess they'd made of the house. The explosion had destroyed anything that might have pointed a finger at Albero. At the same time, it served as a warning for Lily. This was Albero's way of saying he wouldn't stop until she and Luke were dead too.

'Tell him, Mum.' Luke's voice was little more than a whisper from the doorway. 'Or this shit will never end.'

'I can't let you go to prison, Luke. We've withheld evidence in a murder case. We're looking at ten years behind bars at least. The judge won't be lenient with *that* evidence on the table!'

Lily moved to stand in front of him, her hands on his

tightly folded arms. For once, he didn't shrug her off. Instead, he kicked at the kitchen floor with a booted toe.

'Or we could be dead sooner.'

With a sigh, Lily leaned her head against the fragile wall of her son's chest. He was so skinny. She worried he wasn't eating enough. He seemed to be wasting away. In a rare show of affection, he unfolded his arms to place them around her shoulders and drew her in for a hug.

'I'm tired, Mum — tired of living in fear, tired of wondering if it will be my turn next. How will Albero finish me off? I'd rather die knowing I'd done the right thing.'

'*Luke*.' Lily's breath hitched. 'No-one else is going to die. There's been enough of that. We just need to find someone we can trust ... someone who will protect us.'

Even though she knew he was right, the consequences were mammoth. Amidst the fear, she couldn't stem the surge of pride. Luke's maturity sometimes scared her. It saddened her to see a glimpse of the man who'd never had the opportunity to be a boy.

'Give Detective Johnson the diary. I trust him. We have no choice. It's the right thing to do. For us, for Tiny ... and the other boys.' He dropped his arms from around her and turned to leave.

'Where are you going?' The panic was hard to disguise.

Luke turned. 'It's okay. I'm not running away. I'll be

outside at the barbeque with Marty. TJ's put the sausages on and we're in charge of cooking them.'

'Don't —'

'Burn myself. I know.' His smile was a little sad as he flicked his fringe out of his eyes and shoved his hands deep in his pockets.

She let him go, followed him outside to watch until he reached the section of the veranda where Marty was reassuring TJ he knew how to "handle a snag on the barbie". Lily wasn't sure whether to be proud or terrified.

Mark loved the Perth hills at night. The stars shone brighter without the glow of the city lights. The bush was alive with sound, a chorus of creatures of the night. The frog calls merged with the chirping of the crickets, somewhere close a possum shimmied up a tree into its nest. The hypnotic calls of the nightlife blended with the laughter around the table. For a moment, Mark could forget about murder and petty theft, and enjoy the peace.

His thoughts turned to Lily. While she'd relaxed somewhat in the glow of wine, warmth and friendship, he knew by the way her hands gripped the thin wooden arms of the chair her troubles weren't far from her mind. He had to admire her strength. All that had happened in the last couple of months alone would have most women hunched over in a hysterical heap. But not Lily. Lily was holding it together quite admirably. How long could she keep it up before it broke her?

She must have sensed him watching her. The laughter froze on her lips as her eyes met his. For a long moment, she held his gaze across the table, searching until she seemed to find what she was looking for. Mark felt the impact of her acceptance and his heart skipped a beat. Suddenly the cop was at war with the man. While his instinct rejoiced at the hint of a break in the case, his body reacted to the intensity of the woman. *Good God*! Gino Bennetti had not deserved this brave, intelligent, beautiful spirit.

Lily leaned across the table toward him. Still entranced, it took him a moment to process her words.

'We need to talk, Detective.'

'Yes. Now?' He watched the pale skin of her throat ripple gently as she swallowed pride and fear.

'Yes.' She turned to Luke, who'd tuned in to the shift in atmosphere and was watching them both. 'Are you coming too?'

Mark could almost smell the boy's fear as he answered, 'No. I trust you, Mum.'

The words spoke volumes as chatter around the table halted abruptly. TJ stood and began to gather the dishes. The others followed her lead.

'Marty, Luke — you guys get to clear the plates and feed Sarge. Scott, it's your turn to load the dishwasher.'

'Yes, dear,' retorted Scott and TJ cuffed his ear.

'I'll put the kettle on for coffee. Mark, there's a basket on the kitchen bench with coffee and tea in it for the cabin. Perhaps you and Lily could take it up there? I'll make sure the boys stay out of trouble.'

'Thank you.' Lily's words were barely a whisper as she turned to face TJ.

In a moment of understanding, TJ pulled her into a quick hug which Lily returned a little hesitantly at first. Mark watched as Lily relaxed a little more. Yes, the healing process had begun. He smiled and over Lily's shoulder, TJ smiled back with a cheeky wink.

Chapter Four

Lily unlocked the door of the cabin. She paused for a moment to look at her temporary home. It looked comfortable and homely. An open plan living area gave it a light and cheerful feel. A basic kitchen nestled in the far-left corner with a door leading into the garden. To the right, two doors opened onto the bedrooms, one with a double bed, the other had two bunk beds.

Lily made her way toward the room with the double bed. She put the bag of clothes she'd selected from the donation on the floor. Later, she'd hang them in the built-in-robe or fold them neatly into the pine chest of drawers against the wall. Someone — most likely TJ — had placed a vase of fresh roses on the nightstand next to the bed. The glass vase shimmered in the soft light of the bedside lamp. For the first time in years, Lily felt safe.

From the kitchen, she heard the sound of the kettle on the boil, a spoon tapping the side of a ceramic mug. She thought about the man behind those sounds and it felt far too much like the comfort of home. She liked him ... possibly a little too much. What was it they called it when the victim falls in love with her rescuer? How would he feel when she told him the truth? Suddenly, the future stretched before her as dark and gloomy as the past she'd left behind.

'Lily.' Mark's hand came to rest gently on her shoulder. The warmth and comfort of it gave her courage. 'The coffee's ready. Come, let's get this over with.'

She wanted to sink into that comfort, absorb it for a moment, take advantage of the promise it offered. For a moment, she did. She placed a hand on his and leaned against him, absorbing his warmth, his strength, his trustworthiness. His arm snaked around her waist to hug her closer and she closed her eyes. When his lips briefly touched her temple, she sighed ... just a moment longer to enjoy the warmth before she faced reality.

'Yes.' Taking a deep breath, she opened her eyes and moved away from him.

He stepped aside to allow her to pass through the door into the living area. She sank into the two-seater sofa and felt the dip as he sat next to her. How much information was too much? She could only tell him what she knew or suspected, or the little titbits Luke had shared before his father's death. Undecided, she reached for her handbag on the coffee table and unzipped a pocket on the side. For a moment she held the little book of secrets between cold hands, her stomach churning, and prayed she wasn't making the biggest mistake yet.

'Luke didn't talk about what he and his father used to go off and do. At first I thought it was great. I figured they were bonding, something I'd hoped desperately for. That Gino was taking responsibility for his son rather than pretending he didn't exist.'

Mark settled in his seat and cradled the coffee cup in his big hands. Lily kept her eyes on the diary when he said, 'I'm guessing they didn't get along?'

'No. Gino never wanted children. When I fell pregnant with Luke, he changed toward me. We'd been married two years and things were okay. Rocky at times, but everyone said it was normal for newlyweds.'

'But?' Mark prompted when she fell silent.

'I was six months pregnant the first time he hit me.' She felt Mark stiffen beside her as he swore under his breath. Her body remembered the pain while her mind remembered the fear. Her baby ... she could have lost her most treasured gift. Determined to finish the story, she pushed away the dark memory. 'I found out he was having an affair and questioned him on it. When Luke was born, he said the baby couldn't be his. That he'd had a vasectomy. Which was true, but what he'd forgotten is that sperm can be fertile two to three months after.'

'Why didn't he insist on a paternity test?'

Lily sighed. 'If it leaked to the press that a prominent gangland lawyer was questioning the paternity of his child, it would put him in the spotlight. He didn't want that sort of attention.'

'And I'm guessing things got worse?'

'Yes. I'll save you the details and cut to the chase.' The details didn't bear remembering. Dark nights, empty days, painful recoveries and the desperate need to protect her precious son from being beaten too. She took another deep breath. 'He pretty much ignored Luke growing up. The only time he acknowledged him was to beat him or criticise when he did something wrong.'

'What did you do?'

'That's the thing ... I did nothing. I buried my head in the sand, hoping they'd both get over it. That things would change once Luke was able to communicate on his level.' She fanned the pages of the precious little book in her hand. 'And they did change ... for the worse.'

'What happened, Lily?' Mark leaned forward and placed a hand over hers.

'He started taking Luke out to "jobs" with him and I watched my son retreat further into himself. At first I thought it was a stage all teenagers go through, like the one where they don't tell you where they're going or who their friends are. One day, I was cleaning his room and I found this.' She held out the diary and Mark took it from her. 'I knew I shouldn't read it, but by then Luke was a wall of miserable silence. I couldn't reach him anymore and I wanted to know what was going on.'

'What happens if I read this diary?'

Lily tipped her head to rest it on the back of the sofa. 'Luke and I could go to prison for obstructing justice.'

Mark's heart stopped beating as he stared at Lily's face, now deathly grey. Her violet-blue eyes empty. His training nagged him to pore over the new evidence as excitement ripped at his gut and his heart began to pound again. The man in him wanted to take Lily in his arms and hold her, protect her, forget what she'd revealed.

'I promised I'd help you, Lily. I won't renege on the deal.'

'Albero will find us and, after you read the diary, you'll know why. He won't stop until all the evidence is destroyed. If he knows you have it, he'll come after you.'

'I'll be waiting,' Mark assured her, as he settled down to read.

'Mark?'

He turned to find her face inches from his. 'Yes, Lily?'

'Thank you.'

'For what?'

'For everything. For trying to help. For being there when the house was destroyed. You've done what you can for us.' The resignation in her tone tore at his heart.

Chapter Five

I hate him. I wish he was dead. He gave Tiny some of the new shit. Marty almost died from it. He's in hospital now and Tiny's gone to juvie again. I heard him telling that blonde chick Tiny's a waster. I hope nothing happens to him in juvie.

Mark ran a hand over his face and squeezed his eyes shut, trying to block out the images that flashed through his mind. He remembered the day of Marty's overdose far too well. TJ and Scott had found the boys at the Tag Raiders club house. Tiny was dosed up to the hilt and Marty close to death from a seizure.

Slowly the puzzle pieces were beginning to fall into place. But would this new evidence stand up in court? He looked over at where Lily had curled up against the arm of the sofa, exhausted, her head resting on her arms. In sleep, she looked even more like an angel with her soft, blonde hair falling loose around her shoulders. Ignoring the devil on his shoulder that tempted him to reach for her and pull her closer into the comfort of his arms, he turned the page and read on.

Fark! They killed Tiny. Jesus. I don't know what to do. Gino held him down. They made me watch. Nic did it.

Shit! Mark's shoulders tensed and he leaned forward to balance his elbows on his knees. The writing in the diary was shaky and uneven in size. Luke must have written the entry right after Tiny was murdered.

Nic filled the fucking syringe and forced it all into Tiny. His screams. I can still hear them. That blonde, she laughed and made a narky comment. I puked and she laughed. It doesn't matter. Tiny's dead.

Mark shut the little black notebook and stood. Fresh air. He needed to clear the cobwebs and think this through. Sarge lifted his head off his paws as Mark stepped through the front door of the cabin and into the balmy night. It was dark up in the hills. No afterglow of street lamps lighting up the sky like on the flats. Here the only light was that of the stars and the big full moon that glowed through the tree tops.

'Come here, boy.' The dog lifted his bulk and stretched, before padding over for an ear scratch. 'This puts us in a bit of a pickle.' Sarge eyed him with big, sad brown eyes, a frown creasing his furry brow as Mark sighed and pulled his phone from his pocket.

He dialled and waited until a deep, grumpy voice said, 'Do you have any fuckin' clue what time it is, dude?'

'It's not like you need your beauty sleep, Princess. We need to work fast. The stakes in the Bennetti case just went up and it could get a little dangerous. I need you to get your lazy arse to the station bright and early tomorrow morning.'

'Nothing lazy about my arse. Now yours on the other hand ... Question is why?' Mark heard the squeak of mattress springs, followed by the sound of a woman's murmur and Harold's muffled reply. 'Jeannie says it's time you came over for dinner.'

'Tell her only if she bakes that choc mint mud cake I like so much. Now, I need you to read the last few entries in Tiny's diary.'

'I thought that's what you were meant to be doing.'

'I got a little ... side-tracked. Keeping a record seems to be important to the Tag Raiders and I'm holding a piece of the puzzle in my hand — Luke's version of events. I need you to look for anything in Tiny's that clearly links Nic Albero to him before he was kidnapped.'

'Side-tracked ... pfft ... I bet! Always the fuckin' knight in shining armour. Gotcha on the diary. So how is our lovely widow?'

'In a cesspool of trouble, Jonesy. Young Luke is in deeper than we thought. Things are about to get ugly.'

Lily's phone vibrated against her hip. Sleepily, she pulled it from inside her pocket and cracked open an eye to read the text.

I know where you are. They had a nasty fire there not so long ago. It can happen again.

The last remnants of sleep vanished as Lily sat up. Panic gripped her throat. Where was Mark? She felt the seat next to her. The cushions were cold. She stared at the message. Should she answer it? Her finger hovered over the red delete bar. No, it was evidence of harassment. She pressed the home button instead and the screen returned to the wallpapered applications.

The sound of Mark's voice reached her ears, and she followed it to the front door of the cabin.

'Yes, I'll be there in the morning ... Yes, first thing ... Why can't you get your own coffee? Make sure you're ready to go with those notes ... Stop nagging, you sound like my mother.' He paused and chuckled. 'Whatever, big guy.'

Lily leaned against the door frame and folded her arms tightly against her churning stomach. She watched Mark snap his phone shut and push it into his pocket. Hers vibrated again and she pulled it out. The buzzing sound alerted Mark she was there. He turned to face her as she read.

Got txt frm N.

Luke's message chilled her to the bone. Nic Albero's mind games were never subtle and always deadly. *Me 2,* she replied.

DM there with u?

Yes. Relief that Mark was still there eased some of the chill. No matter how angry he was they'd hid evidence from him, justice seemed less scary than the threat of Albero's rage.

Good. Worried. All ok?

She looked up at Mark. His features were tight, his lips unsmiling. *We'll b ok. Fwd N's txt 2 me.*

Yer K. Luv u.

Lily's hand shook as she texted, *luv u 2 xx*

'Lily?' Mark's voice reached her.

Tears burned behind her eyes and threatened to spill over. 'He never says that anymore.'

'Who?'

'Luke. It's the first time in years he's told me he loves me.' The phone buzzed again. She looked at the screen and let the tears fall.

Have snow 4 u. cum n get it. SS sez freebie. 4 ur help with Tiny.

Her heart plummeted. The bastard was deliberately baiting them, making sure they knew he could easily name Luke if they dobbed. What did it matter anymore? There was no way they'd get out of this mess.

Mark stepped closer. She took one last look at the message and handed the phone over. His warm fingers brushed hers as he took it and read the message. She stepped back, stood straight and focused on the soothing sounds of the night.

Mark dropped his hand to his side. 'I won't let him hurt you or Luke, Lily.' He searched her face as she refused to meet his eyes. 'He's panicking now. That's when he'll make mistakes.'

'Text threats are like video evidence. They don't always stand up in court.'

'It's my job to make sure they do. Try to get some sleep. It's been a rough day.'

Lily nodded. 'I'll try.' *I hate that I sound so weak, so needy, so —*

'It's okay to be scared. Perhaps you should stay up at the main house tonight? Sarge and I will walk you over.'

Chapter Six

Lily awoke to the sound of the birds, sunlight peeking through the slats in the blinds. Eyes gritty with lack of sleep, she lay a moment absorbing the peacefulness of early morning. The fear that had gripped her during the night had abated somewhat and acceptance had taken its place. Their future was in the hands of the only man she could trust — the man who held the key to their prison cell.

Enough drama! Lily tossed the sheets aside and edged off the soft mattress. She listened for a moment for sounds of movement around the house, but it seemed everyone was still asleep. Lily tugged on a pair of jeans and T-shirt and padded across the carpeted floor. After a quick pit stop in the bathroom, she slipped quietly into the kitchen.

The morning mist swirled above the hill tops and away toward the sun as Lily looked out the kitchen window. Her gaze caught on a lone chimney stack to the left of the four guest cabins. The sun warmed the weathered stones of the chimney and fell on the fire-blackened soil around it. Curious, Lily unlocked the back door and stepped out onto the veranda. She slipped her feet into the running shoes she'd left at the door the night before.

Slowly making her way up the hill, she took a moment to absorb her surroundings. Nic had mentioned a fire in his text. The scars from it still marred the ground. New grass sprouted enthusiastically from the black soil. Here and there, colourful crocuses grew stark against the hill and around the base of the ruined chimney.

Just like my life, Lily thought. *Hope springs eternal.* Was it a sign, a hint from Mother Nature that things would get better? She bent to pluck a bright orange crocus from the ground and tucked it behind her ear. Lifting her face to the sun, she breathed in the clear, fresh air and let the warm rays stroke her cheeks. *Beautiful.* The heaviness in her heart lifted a little and her fear for the future receded with the mist, even though she knew it would return at nightfall. With a smile on her lips, she hugged her arms close to her chest and opened her eyes.

Next to the old chimney stack sat a cement ornament of an old Holden ute. In the misshapen tray-back, a pot filled with a pretty blue flowering plant languished lazily. Lily kneeled for a closer look. Carved into the cement was a message: *For Tiny, you earned your wings too soon.*

'It's *Lobelia Tenuior* or "Blue Wings".' Lily jumped at the sound of TJ's voice. 'Gosh, sorry Lily, I didn't mean to scare you. Here, I brought you a coffee.'

Lily stood and wrapped her hands around the mug TJ handed her. 'Thanks. For everything.'

TJ shrugged. 'That's the whole point of building the refuge. It's not just for the kids, it's for everyone to make a fresh start. Even Marty's mum comes up on weekends these days. It took time to convince her, but when she realised Marty was serious about going straight, she thought it would be best if she contributed too. She cleans the cabins, does the laundry, and is teaching the girls from the local high school quilting. Soon each cabin will have a handmade quilt. Quite homely, don't you think?'

Lily smiled. 'It sounds lovely. Was there a garden here before the fire? It seems like such a peaceful place.'

'No. It was pretty wild up here. Long grass, random and gnarled old plants from a long-ago garden when there was a cottage around this fireplace.' TJ rubbed a hand lovingly over the warmed bricks. 'We're planning to re-landscape the garden now that we have the cabins built but it's a matter of finding the time and the labour.'

'Did you have anything in particular in mind?'

TJ shrugged again. 'I guess. I'm waiting for inspiration to strike.' She sipped her coffee. 'I don't suppose you know anything about landscaping, do you?'

Lily laughed, a hollow sound in the early morning air. 'I have no idea. Gino hired a gardener to do ours.' Tears pricked and she pushed them back. 'He hired a lot of people to do his dirty work.' Realising, what she'd let slip past her lips, she quickly swallowed a slug of her coffee.

'It's okay, Lily. You can trust me. Scott and I are here to help you. Sometimes it helps to just talk it out.'

Lily sighed. She'd bundled up the feelings for so long. It was hard to voice what she thought. 'I spent the last fifteen years wishing he was dead. Now he is. I don't feel an ounce of remorse, only ... relief. What sort of a person does that make me?'

In the distance, Sarge's bark mingled excitedly with shouts from the boys. Scott's deeper baritone rang out and upped the noise level. The household was awake, yet the peace remained, unshattered. TJ lifted the mug from Lily's nerveless fingers and placed both on the ledge of the old fireplace. Wordlessly, she drew her into a hug. Lily had to lean down a little into it with the difference of a few inches. What TJ lacked in height, she made up for in warmth and for the first time Lily could remember in a long while, it felt good to be hugged. Besides last night, when Mark had held her. That had felt like coming home. Far too comfortable, far too ... right.

'No-one deserves what you went through. It takes time to convince yourself of that,' TJ said, releasing her. 'You are *not* the guilty one. Gino made his choices, and it lost him a beautiful family. It's your turn at happiness now, Lily. Mark will make sure Tiny's killers are caught. He won't rest until he takes them and their drugs off the streets. Luke and Marty have a chance at a new life, and so do the other children we're able to help. We're making a difference, one child at a time.'

'You make it sound so ... possible.'

TJ held Lily's hands in hers, warmth and comfort in the touch. 'It is. I won't stop trying and you shouldn't either. One thing I can promise you is that you can trust Mark. We go back a long way. I've seen him in action more than once, with the boys and their troubles, with Scott and Serena's messy business. Mark has a sister. You might know her name. Peta Johnson was a star born out of the Golden Diva nightclub in Northbridge.' At Lily's nod, she continued, 'One day when we have more time I'll tell you about how he tracked down her daughter's kidnapper. Paul Price would have killed them both if Mark hadn't been so determined to put him away.'

'Oi! You two coming down for breakfast sometime this morning?' Scott yelled from the veranda.

TJ let go of Lily's hands. 'Only if you're cooking it!' She turned and yelled. She turned back to Lily and held out her hand. 'Talk to the man, trust him. Trust us. What do you say? Will you let us help you find your feet again?'

Lily looked at TJ's slender hand. Small hands, neat nails, palms with calloused ridges, a firm yet comforting grip. 'I'll do my best to.' She slipped her hand into TJ's with a smile.

Breakfast was a noisy affair. As Lily stacked the dishwasher, she realised she hadn't laughed so hard in ... well ... ever. Scott's parents, Rose and Bill, had wandered over from their property close by, sometime during the pancake tossing competition. With Sarge happily wolfing down the spoils, Bill was declared the champ. He got to wear the foreman's cap and call the shots for the day. Gleefully, he marched the boys up the path to the shed where they were restoring TJ's Holden Gemini, Sheila. The girls breathed a sigh of relief as blissful peace descended on the kitchen.

'Goodness me!' said Rose, sinking into the chair as soon as the last of the dishes were cleared away. 'I think Scott might have to make the kitchen a little bigger, love. We're going to need more space soon.'

'Yes, we've had plans drawn up to extend the dining area and combine it into the kitchen. We're going to install a catering kitchen too. With a few more volunteers on board now, we'll be able to cater for meals.' TJ wiped the table and turned to rinse the cloth off under the tap. 'The idea is to have it run by volunteers and the residents during the week to free Scott and me up to manage the workshop rehabilitation program.'

'Landscaping, catering, sewing classes — sounds like you need a program coordinator, TJ,' said Lily, popping a dishwasher tablet into the holder and closing the door.

'Ha! You be careful making suggestions, love,' Rose chipped in, 'or before you know you it, you'll be roped in and volunteering.'

Laughing, Lily replied, 'It's not like I have anything else to do. Although I do have a mind to have a go at the garden design.'

'Don't let us stop you. Bill has a potting shed you can raid for tools, if you like?'

'I might do that.' Lily smiled. Excitement flowed through her at the thought of a challenge, even one as simple as creating a garden. Plants meant new life and that's what she needed. Hope for a new life and the challenge of establishing one.

Lily at nineteen, dressed in an ivory satin and lace wedding dress, dreamy-eyed and naïve as she posed for the photo with her groom, Gino Bennetti. Anger stabbed at his gut as Mark studied the photo he'd found folded into the pages of Luke's diary. Hair like spun gold flowed over her narrow shoulders and down to her slender waist. Clear, milky skin and innocent blue eyes, a beautiful young girl far removed from the battered widow he knew.

His heart ached for her. Perhaps because she reminded him of his sister, Peta, who'd been through the same hell before finding the love of her life, Jaime again. Now happily married, pampered and pregnant, they lived comfortably in Perth's suburbs with their ten-year-old daughter, Bella. Mark sighed as he traced Lily's beautiful face with his forefinger. She deserved a second chance too.

Lily had reached in and touched his heart at a level that went far beyond the call of duty though, and that was dangerous. The tug he felt when she was near, the need to fold her into his arms, pick her up, carry her away and adore every inch of her body the way she deserved. To watch her come to life under his hands and to taste those sweet, bow-shaped lips, feel the slide of her silky skin against his ...

'Hey, Lover Boy! Are we going to solve this case or are you planning on wasting time daydreaming?' Mark's head jerked up and he found Harold studying him with narrowed eyes. 'You can't afford to get soft on the widow. You'll get pulled from the case.'

'No shit, Sherlock,' he grumbled. 'Can't get soft on the widow, huh? Is that why you've arranged for your lovely missus to pop in to the refuge and buddy up?'

Harold shrugged. 'I figured she could use a friend. A bit different to the thoughts you were having just then.'

'So, you're a mind reader too now?'

'Didn't have to be. I could smell the testosterone levels rising from here.'

Mark shook his head and smiled wryly. It wouldn't surprise him if Harold had. The man had a nose like a bloodhound and his body's reaction to his thoughts was perfectly normal after all. The last thing he wanted to do was compromise this case or Lily and Luke's freedom. He willed his mind to concentrate on the task at hand.

'Find anything interesting in Tiny's diary, Harold?'

'The kid liked to draw pictures. Good at it too. The graffiti analysts are looking at it now. We should have a full report by the end of the week. Anything interesting in Luke's?'

'A couple of pictures for the analysts but not as heavy as Tiny's. Luke's seems more personal. I'm guessing the drawings are where the clues are.'

'And the fact that the widow and the kid withheld crucial evidence in a murder investigation?'

'Luke is up on charges for his father's death, not Tiny's. So, the evidence they withheld impacts Tiny's case not Luke's. The chief reckons it's not uncommon for the defence or prosecution to fail to turn over evidence that might cast doubt on guilt. In this case, because it was domestic violence, there'll be leniency toward protection of a minor. According to Giles Pritchard, the defence could argue that Luke was as much a victim as Tiny was. We just need a breakthrough. Something that will pin this squarely on Albero, Bennetti and Snow.'

'Serena Snow is the quiet one. I'm wondering if she's the kingpin.'

'We'd still have to prove it.'

'Should we see how much the boy and his mum will tell us without a lawyer present?' Harold suggested after a moment.

'If they know they're not in danger of arrest, I think they'll cooperate. Lily is slowly starting to talk. It's a trust issue but I'm working on it.'

Mark stood and stretched. He'd hunched over Luke's diary all night. His conversation this morning with the chief prison officer had confirmed his suspicions that it wasn't uncommon at all for gang members to conceal secret messages in notebooks. It was common knowledge that tags, and wall art all contained subliminal messages. Tattoos too, he thought, like the one on his left bicep.

Everything had a reason or an explanation — like the connection between Gino Bennetti, Nic Albero and other prominent gangland members he'd managed to link them to, all connected in pecking order with red string on his corkboard. Piece by piece, the puzzle was forming a picture he wasn't sure he liked.

His gaze drifted to the whiteboard where he'd attached a blown-up picture of the hangman Tiny had drawn on the cover of his notebook. So many secrets, so many victims — far too much crime for a group of teenagers to have experienced. And then there was Lily …

'Oh, for fucks sake, Romeo,' growled Harold. 'You've got that dumb-arse dreamy look in your eyes again. Let's drag your horny arse up the mountain and get this over with. Might have to set you up with Jeannie's mother to get you out on a date with a real woman.'

Mark chuckled. Jeannie's mother was ninety in the shade and never passed up the opportunity to pinch his backside. 'I'd marry Olive tomorrow if she'd have me.'

Lily slopped on sunscreen and slapped on a hat before making her way up to the proposed garden with a garden fork in one hand and a basketful of tools in the other. Bill had happily helped her raid his potting shed with the promise of offloading seedlings and mulch later that afternoon.

'Where to start, Sarge?' she asked the dog, who'd followed her up the path. He frowned and padded off to sniff the ground. 'Thanks for the help,' she said when he flopped down in the sand in front of the old chimney and closed his eyes.

Lily looked around, allowing her imagination to take control. After a while, she pulled out a sketch pad and coloured pencils from the basket and began to put her ideas to paper. Half an hour later, she leaned against the warm stone of the chimney and patted Sarge's sleepy head. 'What do you think?'

The dog lazily opened one eye and grumbled. Lily laughed. She'd laughed a lot in the last day and a half, she realised. That deep ache in her heart, that emptiness was slowly starting to subside. For the first time in twenty years, she felt a little safer, despite the shadows that still hung over their heads. Here in the garden, she could heal, forget for a moment what tomorrow might bring as she turned the soil and brought new life to this forgotten space.

She had complete faith in Mark to solve the case and put Albero in prison for good. He still had her phone. Had any more messages come through? He'd taken Luke's phone last night too. The more evidence they had the stronger the case against Albero would be. She didn't need the damn thing anyway.

Could Mark protect them from Albero's threat? Lily looked around her at the devastation the fire had caused.

Had he really done all this damage? Razed cabins in an environment where bush fires took hold too quickly and caused unimaginable devastation, putting people's lives at risk — all to keep his illegal activities a secret. Is that what he'd meant by his reference to the fire last night? TJ had said it was arson and that it was still under investigation.

Lily grimaced as she pulled out weeds and cleared the area around the chimney. On her plans, she'd created a seating area around the fireplace. Maybe one of the boys could get in there and clear the growth and abandoned nests out of the chimney, open it up so that they could have an open fire during the wet season, when there were no fire bans. A gazebo built around it would provide protection against the elements, café blinds that could be dropped to keep out the rain and cold. A guard in front of the fire to keep any dangerous embers from escaping. A peaceful haven to tell stories, share experiences, have fun and heal.

The sun warmed her back and put colour in her cheeks as curious galahs poked around at the bugs and seeds she turned over out of the soil. Occasionally, a magpie would swoop at something shiny, a bottle cap or piece of foil. Geckos slithered up the stone wall of the chimney to bake in the sun. Lily's head lifted at the roar of an engine coming up TJ's steep driveway. Shading her eyes with a gloved hand, she saw it was Mark. Sarge sat to attention and barked.

Apprehension crawled up her spine. This was it, the moment she'd dreaded since she'd found Luke's diary. The moment the truth would come out and change their lives again, just when they were finding a new path. 'It's okay, boy,' she said patting his neck. He whined and nudged her with his nose. She sighed. 'Like everything else, we'll just have to deal with it. Small steps, every day, Sarge.'

Lily looked at the progress she'd made in the garden and prayed she'd be allowed to stay and see it to fruition. She ignored the flutter of her heart when car doors slammed in quick succession. Would Mark be angry with her? Had he come to arrest them? She stood and applied the garden fork to turning the soil, slowly revealing the fresh, undamaged ground beneath. Soon Bill would come, and they would cover it with nutrients, feed it, and nurture it back to health. Footsteps sounded behind her, and the breeze carried the scent of aftershave, a woodsy soap and healthy male. Her heart missed a beat and attraction tugged at her belly as she breathed in the scent she'd come to associate with Mark.

'It's looking good, Lily.' His deep voice shivered over her.

For a moment she wasn't sure whether he meant the garden or the evidence they'd handed over. Choosing the garden seemed like the safer topic. She leaned on the garden fork and turned to look at him, searching his face, gauging his mood. 'Thank you.'

'Is that what you have in mind?' With a reassuring smile, he flicked a hand at the sketch pad propped up in the basket. 'Can I have a look?'

'Sure ... I guess.' The tension in her shoulders eased a little and the knot in her stomach loosened. Surely he wouldn't be making small talk if it was bad news. She had to think positive. It was all she had left.

Mark bent to pat Sarge. 'Some guard dog you are. Lying there and letting strangers walk up unannounced.'

Sarge looked at him with soppy eyes as Mark stroked his head. Lily watched as he scratched the dog's ears, imagined the gentleness in his touch, and found herself thinking what a lucky dog he was. If those big warm hands stroked her hair, her face, she'd turn her face into his palm, plant a soft kiss there. Maybe one at the pulse on his wrist too. For a moment she allowed herself the freedom to dream as his jeans hugged firm and sexy hips, pulled tight across his muscular thighs when he squatted to pick up her sketchpad and ran long, well-shaped fingers over her drawing. She imagined those fingers trailing up her thigh, caressing her hip, cupping her bottom and drawing her against him. Heat flooded her. Parts of her she'd thought long dead tingled with need.

'Lily, these are ——' Mark's words ended abruptly as he stood and caught the burn in her eyes. He closed the sketchpad and put it in the basket then strolled toward her, holding her gaze. 'You shouldn't look at me like that.'

'I'm sorry ... I ...' Her heart beat faster, totally captured by the answering heat in his dark and stormy eyes.

'No, don't apologise.' The warmth of his finger traced her lips. 'I'm attracted to you, Lily. In another time, another place, we might have a chance. Right now, though, there's too much at stake. You're a new widow, a victim, no matter what the circumstances. Earning your trust to treat Luke's case with fairness is far more important to me.'

He was right. Could she trust him? He'd saved her from getting killed, promised her protection, found her a safe haven. Was that nothing but a trick to get her to reveal the information he wanted? And when the case was over, what then?

'I see those questions in your eyes and you're right to be thinking them. Any involvement I have with you now can jeopardise the case, but God help me, I'd like to kiss you right now.' He stepped closer until she felt the brush of his body against hers. 'May I, Miss Lily, just this once?'

She lifted her head, parted her lips, willed them to say no, but the words wouldn't come as her heart shouted yes. Big hands cupped her face, lifted her chin and his head descended to block out the sun.

Warm, firm lips sampled hers, testing her response.

Hesitantly, Lily returned his kiss, tasting a blend of chocolate and mint. With each brush across her mouth, the taste of him drew her deeper. The garden fork clattered to the ground and her hands rested in the curve of his waist to steady herself. Her head spun as he gathered her closer into the cradle of his hips where the effects of their kiss were evident. She revelled in the strength of it and burrowed into the warmth and length of it as she responded to the magic of his lips on hers.

All reasonable thought fled as Mark's hand came up to caress the curve of her back, trailed up and down her spine leaving a trail of desire singing along her nerve ends. She moaned against his seeking lips and lifted her hips to feel his essence at her core. Desperate need she'd never felt before consumed her as her body begged his for attention. A call he answered with equalled passion.

'Ah, Lily,' he muttered against her lips. Slowly easing back and inevitably cooling the passion that simmered between them, he lifted his head. 'We can't do this right now. The case, the timing ...'

'I know,' she answered, enjoying the heat of his body for a moment longer as her hands caressed the unsteady hammering of his heart.

There was no need for apologies or explanation. They felt what they felt. Whether right or wrong, good or bad, it was there and it would be dealt with one step at a time. Like everything else in her life. She pressed a lingering kiss at the V of his shirt that revealed a smooth, golden throat, felt the press of his lips against the crown of her head, missed the warm security of his arms as he dropped his hands and stepped away.

'I'll see you at the house. We have a few more questions for you and Luke.'

'Yes,' she agreed and watched him walk away, a hand on her pounding heart.

Chapter Seven

Lily took her time getting to the house in the hope it would give her heated cheeks time to cool. Wow, what a kiss. She'd felt it to the depths of her soul. Gino had seldom kissed her, even in their early years together. Sex was always hurried. A means to an end and the satisfaction was all his. Propping the garden fork up against the veranda rail, she turned to the garden tap to wash off the soil and soot that had crept in under the gloves. The water was chilly, the pipes not yet warmed by the sun.

No, there'd been no after-sex cuddles or affectionate kisses. No affection at all, come to think of it. He'd be back to business, throwing off the covers, into the shower and out of the house. And it was always morning sex. She could set her alarm clock by his actions. Had she been such an uninspiring lover that

Gino thought it a duty to be gotten over with as quickly as possible?

Stop blaming yourself! It takes two to create the passion. Would Mark be a hurried lover? Or would he take the time to please them both? Lily splashed cold water on her flaming cheeks. It was better not to wonder, not to dream. Whatever was between her, and Mark was best left unexplored. She and Luke had too much to lose, too much to rebuild. Albero's shadow and Gino's ghost still ruled their lives and until they no longer did, she had no right to dream. She wiped her hands on her jeans, whipped off her hat, shook out her hair and hoped she didn't look like a grubby scarecrow.

Taking a deep breath to steady her nerves, she climbed the veranda steps and opened the kitchen door to the noise of an excited dog and the blend of varying tones of male voices. She spotted TJ making coffee and headed for the safety of the oestrogen zone.

'Have fun out there, Lily?'

Lily's cheeks flared. *Oh God*! Had TJ seen them? She hesitated before answering, 'Yes, I did. Turning the soil was quite therapeutic. Although I think I might feel it in my muscles later.'

TJ smiled. 'Wait until you start planting and seeing it come to life. I can't wait to see what you've done in the sketches. I'm sure it's going to look great.'

'Gosh, I really hope so.'

'Bill dropped off a book on native gardens he

thought you might like. He was on his way to the garden centre to arrange a load of mulch for you for the flower beds. He said to have a look and let him know which plants you wanted to start with.' TJ handed her a mug of coffee which she accepted gratefully. 'I think he's keen to give you a hand with it too. He's been looking for a project since we finished building the cabins.'

Pleased that the conversation had taken such a normal turn, Lily felt the heat in her cheeks recede once more. She turned to lean against the kitchen bench and searched for Luke amongst the men. He was chatting animatedly to Harold Jones, his eyes shining with excitement. She caught the odd word. Model aeroplane, 12-volt battery, remote range. Marty stood next to him, nodding with equal animation, his face beaming. Slightly to the left, with his back to her, Scott engaged in a friendly footy argument with Mark.

Lily indulged in a study of Mark from the safety of distance between them. The dark blue, police-issue polo shirt hugged broad shoulders and muscular arms. Her gaze followed the line from his hands, over the strong forearms to the flex of the biceps that stretched the sleeves of his shirt. She lingered there for a moment. How would they feel if she ran her hands over them? Was the body beneath that shirt equally as taut and toned? Yes, she'd felt its hardness against her. Up past the strong throat to a firm jawline and magic lips. Her gaze lingered there for longer than she'd intended as her mind relived the feel of them on hers. Need shot through her like an arrow. The lips twitched under her scrutiny and her gaze shot up to meet twinkling grey eyes. *Busted.*

'Coffee's up! Come and get.' TJ's voice broke the spell as she dropped a packet of Tim Tam's onto the table.

The chatter continued around the table as they drank the coffee and finished off two packets of chocolate biscuits. Lily knew the friendly chatter would end and the real reason the detectives were here would soon be revealed. Did they simply have more questions to ask, or would it be more sinister than that? No matter what simmered between them, Mark's first priority was the case. The outcome of that would determine whether there was a future in what they felt for each other. The moment came before she was ready for it.

'Lily, we have a few questions to ask you and young Luke when you're ready.' Harold Jones drained his mug and placed it in the centre of the table.

'Of course,' she responded, looking at Luke to gauge his reaction. Luke played with the ear of his mug, his face set. 'Luke?'

'Yep,' he responded, not looking up.

'Okay,' said TJ, standing up. She collected the empty mugs, placed them neatly in the kitchen sink and tossed the empty biscuit packets in the trash. 'We'll leave you guys to it. We're up cleaning out the cabins if you need us.'

Mark waited until the door closed behind them before he spoke. 'Luke, we need to know what happened the night Tiny died.'

'Wait!' Lily interrupted. 'What happens to Luke if he tells you what he knows?'

Mark sat back in his chair. 'If we can prove beyond reasonable doubt that Luke is as much a victim in this as Tiny was, then he is purely a witness.'

'And if we can't?'

'We will.'

The assurance in his voice was comforting but Lily knew she wouldn't be convinced until it was over. There was no turning around now anyway.

'Your cooperation with the investigation counts in your favour,' Harold reassured her. 'All we need is for young Luke to tell the truth to back up the evidence.'

'What about protection?' Lily turned to Harold.

'If we can prove that Luke is in danger, he will be given protection.'

'Luke?'

'I want it over, Mum.' He twisted his hands, bounced his right leg nervously and hid behind his dark fringe.

Lily hesitated a moment longer. She looked at Mark, studied his grim face, the set of his lips and the determination in his eyes. She saw beyond the poker face and into the soul of the only man she trusted to keep them safe. 'Then let's get on with it. I've a garden to finish.'

Mark felt the impact of her searching eyes all the way to his groin. She'd drawn back the layers and stared right into his heart. Her trust in him weighed heavily. He couldn't afford to fail her or Luke. And when all this madness was over, he would take her in his arms and —

'Right,' said Harold, cutting across Mark's thoughts. He pulled out his iPad and began to make notes. 'Luke, can you tell me what happened on the night Tiny disappeared?'

Luke slouched in his chair and stretched his feet out ahead of him. In his hands he folded and refolded a serviette with nervous fingers. Lily placed a hand on his and squeezed.

'Gino told me we were going to pick up a package.'

So, Luke called his father by his first name. No affectionate terms for the man who made him. That said a lot about the father-son relationship, Mark thought.

'We went to the convention centre where Tiny was.'

'For the motor industry awards night, right? He was nominated for an award?' Harold asked.

'Yeah, apprentice of the year. He was chuffed. He'd been talking about it a lot and it made Gino mad. Gino said he'd make more money working with them.'

'Working with them?'

'Yeah, running the drugs. Tiny did deliveries too —

drops and pick-ups.' Luke twisted the serviette around his fingers.

'What happened when you got to the convention centre?' Harold prodded when Luke went silent.

'Gino sent me upstairs and told me to wait for Tiny at the toilets. He said to tell him he had a present for him.'

'What did Tiny say?'

'He said to tell Gino to fuck off. Sorry, Mum.' Luke sighed. 'I told him I was scared. That I had a feeling something funny was going on. He said he did too.'

'What happened then?'

Luke shrugged. 'The Hangman came up and took us both to the car.'

Mark straightened in his chair. 'The Hangman?'

'Yeah, that's Albero's tag.'

That made sense. In the graffiti Tiny had drawn in the notebook was a picture of a stick figure hanging from a noose, like the spelling game they'd played as kids. For every word you spelt wrong, a piece got added to the picture until your stick figure hung from a noose and your opponent yelled 'Hangman!' He wondered if kids stilled played that game and if Luke understood the significance of the tag Albero had chosen. 'So, what did the Hangman do?'

'Albero never makes an appearance unless there's major shit. I knew Tiny's time was up. So did he. He couldn't run. There were too many people around.'

'Why didn't he ask for help?

'Albero told him not to make a scene, to come quietly. He didn't want to attract attention, but he would if he had to. We had no choice, we had to go or put the people around us in danger too. Marty was meant to be there, but he stayed in the conference room.'

Mark watched Lily's reaction. Tears warred with the horror in her eyes. How many times had she relived this scene with Luke?

'Go on, son,' Harold encouraged.

'All the way to the park, I kept thinking of ways to escape. I knew the Hangman was pissed off about Marty not coming out. We weren't allowed to talk. Gino drove, I sat in front. Tiny and Albero at the back. At the park it was dark. The lights in the public toilets were out. There was a woman there waiting for us. They called her Snow.'

'Serena Snow?'

Luke shrugged. 'I guess.'

Harold tapped the notes into his iPad. 'Go on.'

'They asked her if she brought the stuff, and she said yes.'

'What stuff?'

'Snow, a mix between Ice and LSD.' Luke shivered. 'It makes you go crazy. You see ... monsters ... weird stuff and feel ... strong, powerful. It makes you mean.'

Lily choked back a sound and Mark stretched a hand across the table to cover hers. He wished he didn't have to put her through this. Hell, he wished *he* didn't have to sit through this, knowing what this poor kid would have witnessed.

Harold paused. 'I know this is hard for you, son. Snow isn't something we want on the streets. Do you need a moment? A drink?'

Luke shook his head. 'No.' He rushed on, the words tumbling over one another in the hurry to get them out. 'They held him down, tied him up. Albero injected him. Too fast. There was air in the syringe. He started to hallucinate, and Snow fed him stories to make them worse until he screamed and begged. He died, paralysed, thinking he was being burnt to death.' The horror of what he'd witnessed reflected on his face, in the tightness of his lips. His features twisting with the agony of the memory, he cried. 'I couldn't do a *fucking thing*. Gino held me, laughing, taunting me, calling me weak and telling me I was next. I yelled at him to stop. He hit me and told me to stop being a baby. I puked. They dragged me to the car. Albero said the same would happen to me if I dobbed.' Helplessly, he turned to Lily. 'I'm sorry. I'm sorry.'

Lily moved closer and took her son in her arms, rocking him like the innocent baby he once was. She pressed a kiss to his head, letting the tears fall as she held him against her heart. 'It's okay, baby. It's all over.'

'I couldn't save him. He was my friend.' Luke sobbed.

Lily held him tighter, stroking his hair as she rocked. 'Now do you understand, Detective? You've seen the lengths Nic will go to — killing children, blowing up houses, death threats — to protect his business. I don't believe we'll be safe in witness protection, but now we have no choice. I want a deal for Luke.'

Mark felt his eyes sting, and his heart grow heavy. What a fucked-up life they'd led. He looked at Harold, who busily tapped away at his iPad, his face unreadable. It was hard, he thought, to sit here and not reach out to comfort Lily and Luke. The best he could do right now was put the culprits behind bars. Problem was, they needed more than two boys' sketches and diaries. They needed hard evidence. The only fingerprints on the syringe were Tiny's. The only evidence that Bennetti and Albero were at the convention centre were hazy security pictures of a car driven by a man whose face they couldn't see ... and a child's word against his own father's.

Chapter Eight

Luke's first day on the apprenticeship program came far too quickly. A week had passed since they'd told their story to Mark and Harold. There'd been no word from Albero, but Lily knew it wasn't over. Albero wasn't stupid. Who knew what tactics he'd try next. Letting Luke out of her sight was the hardest thing to do.

'He'll be okay,' TJ promised, as she held open the door to let Marty and Luke race past. 'We'll keep a close eye on him. He'll spend most of the day doing orientation and filling out paperwork with his counsellor, Ethan Wright.'

'I know. It's just —' Lily spread her hands and shrugged.

'I understand. I'll give you a call a couple of times

during the day and let you know how he's doing. If you're planning on working in the garden today, give Bill a call to give you a hand.'

'Thanks, TJ.'

'You're welcome. Oh, I've left the refuge mobile phone on the kitchen table. Would you mind keeping it on you today? If anyone rings for assistance, let me know and I'll send someone out.'

Lily smiled. In the week they'd been at the refuge, callers had always rung TJ or Scott on their personal mobiles or on the house phone, so Lily knew that leaving her the mobile phone was more about making sure she had a means of contact on her at all times. 'Sure thing,' she said and stayed on the veranda to wave them down the drive.

Eager to get to her garden, Lily pocketed the mobile phone on her way through the kitchen and out the back door. Sarge, ever vigilant and faithful, dogged her steps up the winding pathway. Together, they took a moment to enjoy the peaceful silence.

The garden was laid out to plan with string markers to segregate the beds. Bill, bless him, had started to build the patio over the old fireplace. Four solid jarrah posts stood sentinel, steeped in concrete footings, and the framework for the roof was almost complete.

Soon Bill would start laying the sheets of Colourbond across it and when the decking was done, she would set to work planting a border of Geraldton Wax around it.

They'd discussed building a wall behind the old brick chimney to serve two purposes, one to protect visitors under the roof from the wind, sun and rain, and the outer wall as a graffiti wall.

Not just any graffiti, but a tribute to Tiny and others who came to the refuge for help — a mural of combined creativity, where the kids could express their dreams, fears and reality.

Yes, Lily thought, it would be a way to encourage them to use their talent for good rather than bad. She was itching to get her hands on a paintbrush herself. Sketching the garden had brought back memories of a time, so long ago now, when she'd enjoyed painting and sketching as a hobby.

Perhaps she could do a few oil paintings and auction them to help raise funds for the refuge. And a job. She'd have to think about getting a job soon. Gino's assets were frozen when he died but Lily doubted she or Luke would see a penny from his estate anyway. It was more likely the courts would seize them as proceeds of crime. Yes, a job would be on top of the list. But what?

'How does a woman with no working experience, find a job in this town, Sarge?'

Sarge looked at her with a frown as she picked up a shovel and began to dig at the edge of a cordoned-off area. He grumbled and lay his head on his paws to watch. How indeed? She enjoyed being part of the volunteer group at the refuge, but they couldn't stay here forever.

Sooner or later, they'd have to move. Lily dug deep into the soil to prepare a place for the first rose bush. She mixed in a little fertiliser and topped it with manure before moving on to the next spot Bill had marked with a yellow "x".

Five holes later, her shovel clanged against a solid surface. Sarge's ears pricked up at the ringing noise of metal to metal and he rose to his feet to amble over for a sniff. Lily knelt in the freshly turned ground and brushed away the remaining soil to uncover a square-shaped biscuit tin. Slightly buckled and discoloured from the heat of the fire that had swept across the surface, it seemed otherwise undamaged.

Excitement bubbled in Lily's stomach. What treasure had she uncovered? She fingered the pattern on the lid. Anzac biscuits — not that old. Sarge whined as he sniffed at the box and nudged it with his nose.

'Okay, boy,' Lily said, ruffling his ears. 'Let's have a look inside.'

Sarge barked as she sat, cross-legged on the ground and lifted the tin with gentle hands. Using the prongs of her weeding tool, she wrestled with the distorted lid until it popped free to reveal a resealable plastic bag filled with an array of paper and objects. Lily shivered a little as she carefully pried open the bag and Sarge nudged against her leg.

'What's up, Sarge?' He whined and nudged some more. 'Okay, okay.'

Lily opened the bag and tipped the items out into the biscuit tin. A little packet containing white powder slid from between the papers. She recognised its shape and form instantly. Her heart squeezed painfully in her chest. *No. Oh God, no.* But Sarge's reaction confirmed what she wanted to deny as he nudged the packet into the corner of the tin. Drugs. She shuffled through the papers and found an envelope, thick with banknotes — over a thousand dollars, she guessed by the weight and size. The rest of the content was a mix of faded photos, a USB, childhood drawings and school reports. Her gaze was drawn to a piece of paper bearing the government logo. She lifted it and let it fall open, careful to hold the very edge of the paper so as not to get it dirty. A birth certificate — Tiny's. Cold fingers crept up her spine as she took in the details.

'You miserable *bastard*, Nic Albero.'

Mark and Harold pored over the diaries and made notes as they pieced their case together one step at a time. With the report back from the Graffiti Team, they could identify the messages in the graffiti art and the direction it pointed them in had Mark excited. Greed was always what tripped up criminals in the end.

'So, Albero played lawyer, Gino was the brawn and Madame Snow ran the show. That we knew already. But why did they target Tiny, a foster kid with no record until he met them? How did they even make the connection?' Harold pushed Tiny's diary aside and leaned back in his chair.

'Yes, how did Luke and Tiny become friends?' Mark flicked through the pages of Luke's diary. 'According to Luke, the Tag Raiders formed at school, just a couple of kids mucking around with graffiti. But how did Bennetti and Albero get them involved in drugs? Why would you screw up your own kid? And why choose Tiny as the runner?'

Harold shrugged. 'Maybe because he was a foster child? No ties, no harm?'

'Mmm, my gut is telling me there's something —' Mark broke off as his mobile rang. He looked at the screen and saw the number identified as the refuge. 'Hello, TJ. What have you done now? Another car chase, citizen's arrest, what?'

'Mark, it's Lily.' Mark shivered as her voice flowed over him like liquid gold. 'I've found something.' The liquid turned to lead.

'Tell me.' He listened carefully. 'I'll be right up. Is Sarge with you?'

'Yes.' Lily's voice quavered a little in his ear and squeezed his heart.

'Good, stay put. I'll get there as quickly as I can.' He ended the call and looked at Harold. 'Looks like we have fresh evidence. Lily uncovered a box of Tiny's stuff in the garden. Are you coming up there with me?'

'Nah, you go riding to the rescue. I'll keep plodding through here. Some of us actually work for the taxpayers' money.' He grinned. 'Besides, I can trust you not to get up to any mischief with the widow, can't I?'

'Fuck off! Have the puzzle finished by the time I get back and I might let you go home early.'

'Ha! Sometimes I think Jeannie would rather have you come home early. Thinks the bloody sun, moon and stars shine out your arse!'

'That's because I'm prettier than you.' He picked up his car keys and tossed them in his palm. 'See ya.'

'Keep your hands in your pockets and off the widow,' Harold called after him.

As he drove up the winding road into the hills, Mark thought about how hard it was becoming to do that. Over the weeks they'd been at the refuge, he'd watched as both Lily and Luke had begun to shed the darkness of their past. He found himself spending more time there, being roped into the volunteer roles, and all the time waiting to see Lily smile, to hear her laugh, watch her emerge like a butterfly from chrysalis.

'Damn dangerous ground,' he muttered as he flicked

the indicator switch up to turn left and onto the climbing driveway of TJ's property. Reaching the parking area, he killed the engine and waited a moment. Through the windscreen he saw her up near the old fireplace, sitting on the ground, legs crossed with Sarge's head in her lap. His heart skipped a beat, and he wiped clammy hands on his jeans. 'Very dangerous ground,' he reminded himself and swung open the car door.

Lily stood as he approached and dusted off her shorts. The movement drew his attention to her firm hips, shapely thighs and slim legs kissed by the sun. She twisted around to brush the soil off her bum and Mark's hands itched. He shoved them determinedly in his pockets.

'Hi, Lily.'

'Hey. Thanks for coming up.' She hugged her arms tightly under her breasts and avoided his gaze. With a nod of her head in the direction of the garden behind her, she added, 'I've left the tin next to the hole for you. Did you want a coffee?'

Mark freed a hand from his pocket to rub at the tension in his neck. 'Love one. I'll bring the tin into the kitchen if that's okay?'

Lily nodded. 'Sure. When you're ready.'

He lowered his hand from his neck and reached out to her. 'You okay?'

'Yes.' She stepped out of reach and turned toward

the house. 'Come, Sarge. I'll get you a drink too,' she said and walked away.

Mark watched and rubbed his hand across the tension in his chest. He'd felt the door slam closed on him as she'd retreated into that damned dark place once more. Whatever she'd found, it was serious. With a sigh, he walked to his car to fetch an evidence kit and rubber gloves. Whatever it was, he was about to find out.

In the kitchen, Lily filled Sarge's bowl, placed it on the floor near the door, and walked over to the kitchen bench to put the kettle on to boil. Normal every day actions in her totally abnormal, screwed up world. She arranged the mugs, spooned in the instant coffee and sugar, and waited, listening to the gurgle of the kettle.

Just when things started looking up — just as hope for a future began to flare — Gino's ghost and Albero's threats reared their ugly heads. God damn it, she was sick of it. She sloshed the water into the mugs and slammed the kettle onto the bench, fighting back the tears. Tears of anger at least — not sadness. She licked a spot of boiling water from her hand, not registering the burn of her skin through the burn of anger and hatred that boiled in her gut.

Damn *fucking* Gino to *fucking* hell! She hoped — no, *prayed* — he burnt in Hell for his sins. The spoon clattered against the aluminium as she tossed it into the empty sink. And as for Albero ... bile rose bitter in her throat as her stomach churned, she'd *fucking* see the bastard hanged. Milk splashed across the counter top as her hand shook with rage. She slapped the lid on the bottle and shoved it into the fridge, slamming the door closed with a satisfying *thunk*. No more secrets. No more lies. *Screw* the consequences, it was time for *justice*.

'Lily.' Mark's voice washed over her like soothing oil as she stood facing the fridge, eyes closed, chin jutting out determinedly and her shoulders tensed. She took a deep breath and released it slowly, uncurling white-knuckled fingers from the fists formed at her side.

'I'm okay. Angry, but okay.' She felt his warmth against her body and willed her shoulders to relax under the comfort of his hand. For a moment, she absorbed the warmth, the comfort, the promise his touch held. Placing her cold hand over his and squeezing lightly, she said, 'Thank you.'

Lily turned under his hand. For a moment she looked into his eyes, traced the lines of his face before she placed her hands on his firm, slender waist and stretched up to meet the lips that had already begun the descent to hers. She felt Mark brace a hand next to her head against the fridge but didn't register much more as his lips warmed her cold ones and the anger drained away to be replaced by something else.

No less consuming, desire flooded through her as she kissed him with all the passion and pent-up emotion she'd stored in her heart for far too long. Her hands wandered from his waist, up over his chest, across his shoulders and into his soft, short blond hair as she pressed into him and dragged him closer.

With a groan, he spread his legs to accommodate her weight, released his hold on the fridge to grip her bottom and pull her closer still. Lily revelled in the heat of his body against hers and stretched against him like a satisfied cat. She rubbed her leg up the side of his in invitation, heat pooling through her as he ran a hand over her thigh and hooked it around his waist. As he lifted her against him, she hooked the other leg up and hoisted into his arms, buried into his chest and sunk even deeper into the magic of his kiss.

'Lily,' he whispered, abandoning her lips to press heated kisses against her neck, into the V of her t-shirt where he nipped at the swell of her breast.

Lily abandoned all reasonable thought even as alarm bells rang in her head. She thrust her hips against his, riding the long hard length of his body, her hands clenched at his nape as she held his lips to her breast, her back against the cold stainless steel of the fridge, eyes closed as she absorbed a pleasurable passion she'd never experienced before. The alarm bells continued to ring, and she ignored them, dragging his lips to hers, desperately seeking the comfort, the promise of loving and being loved in return. But the damn bells wouldn't stop ringing. Realisation penetrated the haze as she felt Mark pull away, slowly, reluctantly.

'Your phone is ringing.' He slipped it out of her back pocket and handed it to her, before slowly letting her slide the length of him.

The phone stopped and he held her against his chest for a moment longer, pressed a kiss on her crown. Breathless and wanting, she stayed there until the phone rang again.

Chapter Nine

'Lily? My God! Are you okay? I've been ringing and ringing. Is Bill there with you? Are you out in the garden?' TJ's voice was frantic with worry.

'I'm okay, sorry. I ... I didn't hear the phone ring.'

TJ let out a sigh of relief that echoed through the phone. Lily looked up at Mark. He towered over her, eyes closed, forehead against the arm he rested on the fridge and the lips that had plundered hers so warmly only moments before, were now drawn in a tight line. She slipped out from the haven his body created and faced reality.

'Mark's here. I found some of Tiny's stuff buried in the garden.'

'Really? Wow! Like what?'

'Some papers, photos, more drawings, that kind of

stuff.' She turned around to watch as Mark pushed away from the fridge and sat at the table to sip at the coffee. The strong fingers that had caressed her body pressed briefly into his closed eyes as if warding off a headache. 'Mark's going to look through them now.'

'Okay. You sure you're okay? You sound a little ... shell-shocked.'

'Yes, it's all good.' Mark's head lifted and his eyes met hers. She smiled tentatively and he smiled back. Her heart lifted a little. 'All good. Everything okay with Luke?'

'Yes, he's having a ball messing around cleaning engine parts and emptying rubbish bins.'

Lily laughed. 'That has to be a first! Emptying rubbish bins. Did you want me to cook dinner tonight?'

'Would you? You angel! We're having a toolbox meeting after work. We have two more recruits for the apprenticeship program, so I need to find another technician and we have to look at installing more equipment.' Excitement rang in TJ's voice.

Lily loved the passion that TJ showed for her rehabilitation project. It warmed her heart that there were people like Scott and TJ ... and now Mark too ... who were prepared to give kids like Luke, Marty and Tiny a second chance, without judging them by their pasts.

'Of course I can. Lasagne and salad sound okay? I might have a go at baking some fresh bread to go with it. Bring home a list of the equipment you need, and I'll phone around for quotes for you tomorrow,' she offered.

'Seriously? You are a legend!'

'I think it's time I earned my keep around here,' Lily joked as she wandered over to the kitchen window to look out at the garden. It was taking shape so nicely, despite the secrets it kept hidden. A sense of achievement flowed through her.

'Oh, I think you're already doing that well enough. How would you like a couple of days work here at the office? I need someone to plan rosters and training programs now that the apprenticeship program is starting to fill up,' TJ asked.

Lily's heart lifted a little more. A real job, a new start — another chance at getting out of the darkness, how could she refuse? 'When do I start?'

TJ gave a loud whoop and Lily held the phone away from her ear. Behind her Mark chuckled and her stomach did a little flip flop.

'We'll talk about it tonight over dinner. Ask Mark if he wants to stay. Tell him Harold and Jeannie are invited too. Rose and Bill too, of course. Can't forget the in-laws, can I? Oh wait, is that okay? You're cooking.'

Lily laughed. 'Of course, no problem. I'll handle it.'

'Right. Gotta go. See ya.'

The phone beeped as TJ rang off and Lily closed the flap. She turned from the window and sat opposite Mark at the kitchen table. He flipped through the contents of the tin, spreading them out on the table in individual plastic zip lock bags. She watched the movement of his hands, trailed her gaze up the strong arms, flicked over his throat where his Adam's Apple bobbed when he swallowed and eyed the smooth curve of his jaw, the full lips ...

'Stop that, Lily.'

The heat in the look he sent her had her squirming. He was right. As much as she'd like to take up where they'd left off, now was not the time or place to explore what lay between them. Hormones — purely hormones. A sex-starved wife, now an equally sex-starved widow, tempted by an undeniably sexy man who happened to be a little tempted himself. A severe case of hero-worship? Some kind of post traumatic bonding with her rescuer? Too many questions and not enough answers. She shrugged.

'Okay,' she said, sipping her coffee.

'Okay? Oh, honey, it's *far* from *okay*.' Mark shifted uncomfortably on the chair. He kept his eyes on the table as he pulled at the legs of his jeans.

Lily smiled. Why shouldn't she enjoy having that effect on a man? God knows, she hadn't had that effect on Gino since the early days of their relationship and even then she wasn't sure he'd ever wanted her with the same passion. Whatever happened next, at least she felt *alive*. There was light at the end of the tunnel at last. She just needed to keep reaching for it.

'What happens now?' she asked.

'With what, love?'

She shivered a little at the endearment, but Mark was so focused on the piece of paper he held in his hand, she didn't think he'd realised he'd used it.

'With the birth certificate.'

Mark took his time to answer as he stroked the plastic covered emblem with a long finger. Finally, he looked at her and smiled — a heart-stopping grin that had her hormones bouncing into the darkest corners of her libido and seared her butt to the chair.

'We go to war to win the fight.' He pushed back his chair and stood, stuffing the contents of the resealable plastic bags into the biscuit tin and forcing on the buckled lid. 'I need to get these to the station and log them in as evidence. I'm surprised Harold hasn't rung already to see what we've found.'

'TJ invited you for dinner. She said to tell Harold and Jeannie too.'

'Sure. What time?'

Lily shrugged. 'About seven-thirty?'

'Okay.' He looked at her for a moment, promise in his eyes. *When this is over ...*

'I'll walk you to your car. Sarge!' she called and scratched the dog's ears as he padded to her side.

She stood and followed Mark out the door, down the veranda steps and to the car. He pressed the button on his remote key, opened the door and dropped the tin on the passenger seat. Straightening, he leaned his arms on the door frame and looked at her.

'See you at seven-thirty then,' he said. Lily nodded and chewed her lip. He reached out to brush her lips with his finger and Lily stilled. 'Screw it!' he said, stepping around the door and gathering her in his arms where he proceeded to kiss her until her legs buckled with the heat of it and her mind fogged with the force of it before he got in the car and drove away.

Lily stood, rooted to the spot, staring at the tail lights of his car as they disappeared down the drive. 'Well ... *Hell*!' she said to Sarge, who groaned and flopped down in the sand.

Mark dropped the biscuit tin on his desk with a satisfied clang.

'Hope those biscuits are fresh,' said Harold, looking up from his computer screen. 'Looks like they've been in the pantry a while.'

'Funny man. This is better than your grandmother's best shortbread.'

'You obviously never tasted Nan's baking. Is that the parcel from the widow?' Harold sat back and stretched. 'It had better be a chocolate cake at best.'

Mark grinned. 'Better than chocolate.'

'Only thing better than chocolate is sex. Oh wait,

that's right. You wouldn't know. You're not getting any, are you?'

Mark pried the lid off the tin and spread the evidence bags across his desk without answering. Harold pushed back his chair and stood to walk around to where he could see the contents. Ignoring him, Mark pulled a large brown envelope out his drawer and began cataloguing the bags in the list on the front. He slapped at Harold's hand as he picked up the packet containing the birth certificate.

'Leave it until I've written it up.'

'Hell no! This looks like interesting reading.' He turned the packet over and studied the names on the certificate. 'Well, fuck me!'

'No thanks, you're not my type.' Mark tossed the resealable plastic bag containing the photos into the envelope.

'Yeah well, lucky for you I like my women with boobs. So Albero's a daddy and whaddya know ... who's your mama! Pricks like that shouldn't be allowed to breed. Poor bloody kid didn't stand a chance with a snow queen for a mother and shark for a father.'

'Tell me about it. Gives the case a whole new spin doesn't it?'

'Indeed. I wonder what's on the USB. A smart kid like Tiny would probably have hooked up the camera on his phone to record stuff. So, what is it, then?' Harold grinned at him.

'Well, you can't look at it until we've logged it all, and will you stop jumping around like a fucking jack-in-the-box? What is what?'

Harold stopped tapping his feet. 'What exactly is your type?'

Mark looked at him squarely and replied, 'A petite, blonde and encumbered widow.'

'That's dangerous ground.' The grin turned into a frown.

'Tell me about it. All the more reason to get this damn case solved and I can take a holiday somewhere on the other side of the world. Forget about teens, drugs, policing and petite blondes with baggage.' He took the bag from Harold's hands and wrote it up. 'Maybe by the time I get back from the Caribbean, she'll have freedom and a new life, and she'll have forgotten about the detective who rode to her rescue. Maybe she'll hook up with Luke's program counsellor. I heard he's single. Can you subpoena Tiny Watts's hospital records from the maternity unit in Port Hedland? I'll need them first thing in the morning.'

'Yes, dear. Ooh! Is that the colour of jealousy I see steaming out your ears?' Harold flicked a finger and thumb against the crown of Mark's head. 'Let's solve this case. What's the next step?'

'We get Albero in for a little afternoon tea and chit chat. By the way, you and Jeannie are invited to dinner tonight at the refuge. Lily's cooking.'

'Nice! What time?'

'Seven-thirty. Are we bringing Albero in or are we going to pay him a visit?'

'Let's pick up some pig slop and pay him a visit. Slimy bastard would use his courtroom skills to avoid coming in anyway. This way we can surprise him.'

Mark grinned. 'Oh, I think he's going to be very surprised.'

Chapter Ten

'I'm sorry. Mr Albero is busy right now.' The slim, pretty receptionist looked more at home in front of a camera than behind an office desk as she placed the telephone handset in its cradle with a perfectly manicured hand. She fluttered long, false eyelashes in Mark's direction. 'He asked if you would please make an appointment and come at a more convenient time.'

Patiently, Mark leaned over the desk, placing his hands firmly on the edge. 'I don't think Mr Albero understands the importance of our visit.'

Pouty lips pursed as she leaned forward. Her too-firm breasts curved invitingly in his direction. 'I can fit you in early tomorrow morning?'

Mark ignored Harold's snort of laughter. 'Perhaps

you can ring him and ask him if we need to come back with a search warrant?'

'Fuck the search warrant! Come on, Lover Boy,' said Harold as he marched over to Albero's office door. He pounded on the door until Albero opened it and when he did, Harold pushed past him into the plush space and looked around. 'So, crime really does pay!'

'I really hope you have a damn good reason for this.' Albero stepped aside to allow Mark to follow before he closed the door behind them. 'I'd hate to slap a harassment suit on our boys in blue.'

'Knock yourself out. You're dealing with a different division now. Since you're such a busy man ...' Harold wandered over to the desk and picked up a copy of the latest edition of Chic Caress. He showed the page to Mark. The statuesque model on page three posed invitingly on a seventies-style shaggy rug. '... we won't keep you long.'

Albero whipped the magazine from Harold's hand and shoved it into his top drawer. 'Sit down ... please.'

Mark eyed the expensive leather chair. Legal advice in the underworld must pay well, he decided as the rich smell of cologne drifted across the desk to blend with whiff of tanned hide.

'Mr Albero, as you know we are continuing the investigation into Tiny Watts' death,' said Mark.

'I thought it was suicide.' Albero sat and lounged in

his chair. 'Bloody kids don't know what they're getting themselves into when they touch that stuff.'

'We have some new evidence that suggests the drug overdose wasn't an accident.'

Albero sat forward and linked his hands on his desk. 'So?'

Mark sat. 'Gino Bennetti's son, Luke, and Tiny were part of the same gang.'

Albero fiddled with the papers on his desk. 'So what?'

'So, we were wondering how well you knew Tiny Watts?'

Albero's hands stilled. 'He was a kid Luke met at school. He went over to Gino's house sometimes. That's as much as I know about him.'

'So, you didn't know he was homeless?'

Albero sat back and linked his hands over a growing paunch. 'What does that have to do with anything?'

'We're trying to trace his parents,' Mark said, watching Albero's reaction. Nothing. 'How did Gino know Serena Snow?'

Albero shifted in his seat. 'You're wasting my time. Get to the point.'

'We have evidence of you threatening Gino Bennetti's widow and sending suspicious texts to her son. You might want to be a little patient here, Albero.' The edge in Harold's voice suggested his own patience had run out. 'What is the connection with Serena Snow?'

'How do you know those calls and texts came from me? My phone was stolen about a month ago.'

'How convenient. Snow and Bennetti?' Harold stood now and leaned toward Albero. A large fist closed around a tie that screamed bad taste, dragging Albero forward in his chair. 'Didn't you get the memo that paisley went out in the seventies?'

Albero pushed Harold's hand away. 'That's harassment, Detective Jones.'

Mark sighed. 'Let go of the tie, Harold. It's ugly and you're not playing fair. Answer the question please, Mr Albero.'

Albero adjusted the knot and smoothed his tie. 'We were in business together a few years ago. Owned shares in a nightclub. That's not a crime, is it?'

'Interesting. What was the name of the nightclub?' Harold sat.

'Relevance? It doesn't exist anymore. Went bang.'

'Things seem to do that around you. What was the nightclub called?' Harold pressed.

'The Golden Diva.' Albero's gaze flicked to Mark's face. 'I'm sure you know it well, Detective Johnson.'

Mark's heart dived and acid churned in his stomach. He fought to keep the emotions from his face even as his hands gripped the arms of the office chair, knuckles white. The Golden Diva, the nightclub that had made his sister, Peta, a star, owned by her ex-husband, Paul Price, until he'd sold it off in shares to pay for his gambling and drug addictions. *Jesus!* He hadn't seen that coming.

Lily danced and sang her way around the kitchen as she prepared dinner. Her homemade pasta sheets, layered with bolognaise mince, parmesan and béchamel sauce baked away in the oven, filling the kitchen with delicious aromas. She pulled the Tiramisu from the fridge and put the finishing touches on it. After putting it away again, she looked at her watch. Plenty of time. What to do next?

Keeping busy would keep her mind off that searing kiss Mark had delivered as he'd left this morning. No good could possibly come from starting a relationship with the man who held your shaky future in his hands. But *oh God* could he kiss! Her lips tingled just thinking about it. Lily wiped her hands on her apron.

The glitter of diamonds in the sunlight streaming through the kitchen window drew her attention and she lifted her hand. Her wedding ring. She still wore it. Why? Stretching her hand out, she studied it. Opulent, designer, brag-worthy ... typically Gino. He'd pressed it onto her finger with promise in his eyes on their wedding day. It hadn't taken long for promises to turn to lies.

Lily tugged at the ring and pried it off her finger. She held it up to the light. It was time to take the final step to severing her ties with the past. The ring should fetch a fair price. Perhaps even enough to find her and Luke a place of their own. Now she had a job — thanks to TJ — they could afford it. It was the least Gino could give them post-mortem. Yes, first thing on Saturday morning she'd borrow a car and go and get the ring valued.

Curling her fingers around it and tucking it into her palm, she turned the oven on low and walked out the kitchen door across to her cabin. In her bedroom, she wrapped the ring up in a tissue and hid it deep inside the pocket of a winter coat she'd retrieved from the donations bundle. Sarge flopped at the side of the bed and eyed her curiously.

'A new start, Sarge. Our own place, our own life.' She patted his head. 'Now you stay here and keep an eye on it for me while I shower and change.'

Sarge lay his head on his paws and waited as she headed for the bathroom. Ten minutes later, Lily stood in front of the mirror, dressed in skinny leg jeans and a cross-over tunic top, stroking mascara onto her lashes.

'What am I doing, Sarge?' She sighed, tossing the mascara tube into the make-up bag. 'Prettying up for what?' She stroked the sides of the pistachio-coloured tunic across her hips. Her eyeshadow matched it perfectly. Lipstick in hand, she shrugged. *What the hell.*

She'd come this far, and she certainly felt better for it. Perhaps a good haircut was in order too. That was one for the list of things to do with her first pay cheque.

She brushed out her honey-coloured hair until it shone like spun silk and fell softly between her shoulder blades. Slipping on a satin head band to match her top, she adjusted the little bow on the right. There. Gone were the traces of Liliana, the battered wife and tragic widow. All that remained as a reminder was the little white scar on her cheek and the wedding ring waiting to be pawned. 'We're moving on without you, Gino.' Turning away from her reflection, she called to Sarge, 'Let's go, boy.'

As she headed to the house, she spotted Scott and TJ's SUV coming up the drive. Lily watched as Marty and Luke spilled out the doors almost before Scott hit the brakes.

'Oi!' he yelled. 'What have I said about waiting until the car stops?'

'Jeez, Scott! I stink like grease 'n shit. Thought you'd be glad to get me off the seats before the smell sticks. Can't wait to hit the shower,' Luke yelled.

Lily's heart warmed at the happiness in his reply. Apparently stinking like "grease 'n shit" was a badge to be worn with honour. 'Hey Luke,' she greeted as he walked past her to their cabin.

'Hey Mum! I'm starving! What's for dinner?'

'Lasagne, and Tiramisu for dessert.'

'Sweet! Hey, Mum, can we like ... talk ... later?' His smile slipped a little and for a moment, the haunted look was back in his eyes.

Lily hesitated. 'Sure. Everything okay?'

'Yeah, just some ... you know ... things.'

'Of course. Mark and Harold are coming over for dinner. When everyone's gone, we'll have a chat.'

For another moment, Luke hesitated as if debating the presence of the detectives. 'Yeah, that's cool,' he said as he walked away.

A sense of foreboding lying unsettled in her stomach, Lily turned to greet TJ. 'How did it go?'

TJ smiled. 'He took to it like the proverbial duck. I think he's going to fit right in.'

Lily let out a sigh of relief. 'Thank you, TJ. I'll go and get things ready for dinner. Rose and Bill will be over soon. When I rang, they were in the greenhouse grafting roses for our garden. Mark, Harold and Jeannie will be up around 7:15.'

'Sounds great! Ready for that shower, Scott?' TJ's eyes twinkled as her husband crossed the veranda toward them.

Scott pulled her close and nuzzled her ear. 'You smell like grease 'n shit too. Let's get you cleaned up.'

Lily watched with envy as they entered the house, already so wrapped up in each other that the rest of the world faded away. It would be so nice to be loved like that. To be cherished and held close and adored for simply being *who* you were. Perhaps when all this was over, she could dream of being loved so completely. With a sigh, she went inside to check on her lasagne.

Sometimes the shit just kept coming quicker than you could connect the dots, Mark thought as he drove up the hill to Karalee. Albero's bombshell had stirred up leads on a cold case he wanted solved more than he wanted a cold beer right now. What a miserable bitch Fate was that she'd found it necessary for these two cases to have a common denominator.

Bennetti and Albero had kept their involvement in The Golden Diva very quiet and pulling cold case evidence from the archives was the last thing Mark had expected to be doing that afternoon. The memories those dusty boxes brought with them had scarred his heart and mind badly enough for him to consider retiring from the force. If it wasn't for Harold talking him out of it, he might have been sailing the Pacific instead right now.

His sister — Peta — battered and beaten, just like Lily. His gorgeous niece, Bella ... missing. And his best mate, Jaime — shot — caught up in the web of lies and deceit that surrounded The Golden Diva.

Mark pulled up in the parking area at the refuge and checked his phone for the umpteenth time. Still no word from Peta. With a sigh, he got out the car, climbed the veranda steps and knocked. Beyond the door, the dinner party was in full swing. He could hear the boys' raspy voices mingling with those of the adults. Harold and Jeannie were here, and judging by the laughter, so was Jeannie's mum. Olive was bound to lighten his mood.

The door swung open and there was Lily. Beautiful, flushed with laughter, small and warm, she held out her hand to take his and draw him inside.

'You're late. Olive was telling us about the hot date you two had.'

Mark smiled and rolled some of the tension from his shoulders. 'Good old Olive. Not the retirement home ballroom dance again?'

Lily picked up on the tired note in his voice he'd failed to hide. 'Everything okay?'

He squeezed her hand in his. 'It will be. Dinner smells good. I hope I'm not too late?'

Lily studied him with narrowed eyes, taking in every inch of his face. 'No, we waited for you. Are you sure you're okay? You look tired ... worried.'

He cupped her face and stroked her cheek with his thumb. 'The case took a bit of a twist today. I'm waiting for a phone call.'

Lily sighed and pressed her cheek into his hand. 'Will it ever be over?'

'Oh, honey, I hope so. Sooner rather than later too.' She stood closer now, so close he could feel her warmth radiating against him, smell her fresh perfume. His body rose to the challenge of hers and he pulled her closer still. 'Lily ...'

'Well, it took you bloody long enough to get here!' Harold's voice had them jumping apart. 'Olive's dying of a broken heart. She thinks you stood her up.'

Mark acknowledged the warning message in Harold's eyes. *Hands off.* He pushed them into his pockets as Lily walked away toward the kitchen. He wasn't sure he could keep his eyes off her either.

'There you are, Mark! I was just telling Lily here about your moves.' Ninety-two-year-old Olive shuffled over and wrapped her arms around his waist, making sure she grabbed a handful of his arse before hugging him.

Mark laughed and gathered the lavender-smelling bundle of woolly jumpers in his arms. 'Olive, my darling, when are you going to put me out of my misery and marry me?'

'Ha! I'm more woman than a boy like you can handle. Besides, that one over there is much prettier than me and *she* can cook.'

'No-one's prettier than you, Olive,' said Mark, releasing her to guide her to a chair.

'No bloody wonder you're still single,' muttered Harold. He dodged the jab of his mother-in-law's cane. 'Blind as a fucking bat.'

'Watch your language! There's a lady present,' Olive warned.

'You're a lot of things, but you're sure no bloody lady,' retorted Harold, his voice softening as he kissed her on the head. 'Can we eat now?'

It didn't take long for the lasagne to disappear. As delicious as the meal was though, Mark couldn't relax. Between the tantalising smell of Lily's perfume and waiting for his phone to ring, his nerves were stretched to the limit. That Olive kept catching him in the act of staring at Lily didn't help either. With a chuckle, she leaned over and squeezed his knee with a knobbly, arthritic hand.

'You've got the hots for her,' she whispered.

'You're the only woman in my life, Olive.' He squeezed the hand on his knee gently. 'How's the arthritis behaving?'

'Don't try to distract me with your pretty words. Are you going to make a move on her?'

Mark sighed with relief as his phone rang. Removing it from his pocket, he glanced at the screen. 'Excuse me a moment, love.' He rose from the table with an apologetic wave. 'Hey,' he said into the phone as he walked through the kitchen door, out onto the veranda.

'Sounds like you're having a party. Finally decided to get a life?' Peta's voice soothed his erratic nerves.

'Something like that. I've had to reopen your case.' Silence dropped like a stone. 'I'm sorry, Sis.'

Peta sighed. 'I'm sure you have a good reason for it. What's happened?'

'A case I'm working on appears to have a common link. Did that ratbag ex of yours ever mention the names Albero, Bennetti or Snow?' Mark wandered over to the veranda to look out over the velvety black sky. A cloud wandered aimlessly across the moon, and he shivered. His gut feeling had run riot all afternoon with a sense of foreboding.

'Serena Snow?'

His stomach churned. 'Yeah.'

'Now that's a name I haven't heard in a while and was hoping never to hear again. She's bad news, Mark.' The tension in Peta's voice increased. 'Will we need to come to Perth?'

'I don't know yet. What can you tell me about her?' He closed his eyes, not really sure he wanted to know.

'She was a regular at the Golden Diva. I caught her dealing drugs and told Paul to get rid of her. He refused and I paid the price for asking.'

'Was there ever anyone else with her other than buyers?'

'Not usually, but after I spoke to Paul about her, two beefy-looking characters started coming in with her. Paul said they were her lawyer friends.' Peta hesitated. 'I was told not to ask any more questions after that.'

'Did you know Paul had two partners in the club?' Mark rubbed a hand across his jaw.

'No. He borrowed money from somewhere which is what landed his sorry arse in prison. I'll never forgive him for what he did to Bella.' The pain in his sister's voice echoed the stab in his heart.

'Should've killed the bastard while I had the chance,' Mark muttered.

'It wouldn't have solved anything. You know that. It would have brought you down to his level. Why did you ask about the partners?'

'Albero and Bennetti. Albero tells me they owned shares. Bennetti can't back it up either way. He's dead.'

Peta's cynical laugh echoed in his ear. 'Is that the reason you need to reopen the case?'

Mark sighed. He turned around to see Lily moving around the kitchen clearing plates away. Through the window, he watched as the light glowed behind her, framing her in a hazy halo. His heart skipped a beat as she caught him looking, answered her wave with a wiggle of his fingers and willed his pulse to slow.

'Yes. I want these bastards behind bars. They've done too much damage already.'

'Really? And that damage ... would it have something to do with a honey-blonde widow and TJ's teenage rehabilitation program?' Peta's voice held a smile.

'Jesus! Do you know everything? Bloody Harold's been shooting his mouth off again, hasn't he?'

Peta laughed. 'Settle down, big brother! Or I might think Harold's right and you do have a crush on the lady in question.'

'It's complicated. How's Bella and the new bub?'

'Changing the subject won't get you off the hook. Bella is fine and the new bub is baking nicely. Speaking of which, I need to pee. Are we done?'

Mark sighed. 'For now. I'll be in touch. Hey, Sis?'

'Yes, I know. Take care of myself and look out for signs of bad guys. I'll let Jaime know.'

'Good. Tell him to watch out for black sedans and slimy lawyers named Albero.'

'Okay. You take care too. Love you.'

'Love you too.'

Mark hung up and turned to stare across the darkened valley. He didn't like the turn the case was taking. They had to find the missing pieces of the puzzle fast.

Chapter Eleven

'Everything okay?' Lily asked from the doorway to the kitchen. Sarge nudged past her and loped across the veranda.

Mark pushed away from the rail and leaned down to scratch Sarge's ears. The big dog leaned blissfully against his legs. 'Yeah, all good.'

Lily stepped over the threshold and moved toward him. 'TJ's making coffee.'

'Thanks.' He straightened to settle his back against the rail as she stepped closer. 'I hate to turn this back to business, but did Gino ever mention a man named Paul Price or the Golden Diva?'

Lily shook her head. 'Gino was always careful not to name drop. I remember him going to a function at the Golden Diva once or twice, though. Why?'

Mark sighed. He raised a hand to brush her cheek with his fingertips. In the moonlight she seemed almost ethereal. The golden glow of her hair, the soft whisper of her voice, the smell of her perfume as the scent tantalised his senses and teased his body. Temptation he dared not succumb to ... yet. He dropped his hand and rammed it into the pocket of his jeans.

'That was my sister on the phone.' His eyes held hers. 'A little over twelve months ago my niece was kidnapped by Peta's ex-husband, Paul Price, and held to ransom for information Peta had gathered on Price's illegal business activities. Price owned the Golden Diva. Peta remembers Serena Snow being there, dealing drugs and Albero told me this afternoon that he and Gino were silent partners in the club.' He watched her face as Lily processed the information. Realisation, anguish, pain, shock — expressions flitted across her features in the glow of the moon.

She reached out a hand to steady herself on his arm as the force of those emotions rocked her on her feet. 'My *God*, Mark ... is there enough evidence to bring them all in?'

'Price is already in prison, but we missed the connection to Albero. We need to make sure where it stops first. We have the trump card with the things of Tiny's you found, but I need to make sure that the net has captured all the bloody sharks before we drag it in.'

Anger coloured his tone and fed his restlessness. He pushed away from the rail and paced, missing the warmth of her hand on his arm.

'Mum?' Luke's voice sounded from the doorway.

Lily turned toward him. 'Luke?'

'Can we have that talk now?'

'Sure ... umm ...'

'It's okay. Detective Johnson needs to know too.' Luke stepped out on the creaky boards of the veranda. 'The Hangman was at work today. He drove into the car park and waited a while. Just watching.'

'Did you let TJ or Scott know?'

Luke shook his head. 'When he saw me throwing away the rubbish, he just kinda laughed and drove off.'

Mark caught Lily's eye and saw the fear there, in the rigidity of her spine and the set of her shoulders. 'Anything else, Luke?'

'Nah, but a little later someone else drove by and stopped for a look.'

'Did you see who it was?' Lily stepped closer to Luke.

'I think it was Snow, but I couldn't see very well. The tint on the car windows was too dark.'

'Good job, Luke. You did the right thing by telling us. I'll let Scott and TJ know to keep an eye out. Whatever you do, don't ever approach the car or either of them, okay?' Mark patted Luke's shoulder. 'Is that all?'

'Yeah.'

Lily watched as Luke turned and walked into the kitchen. She waited until she heard him talking to Marty before she turned to face Mark.

'I'm scared, Mark. Scared for Luke. If anything happens to him ...'

'Nothing's going to happen, Lily ... to either of you. I promise you that.' He stepped closer, placed a comforting hand on her arm. The skin was soft and silky under his, if not a little chilled. 'Trust me when I say I want these guys as badly as you do. For you, for Luke and for my own family ... and I won't give up until I have them all.'

'I trust you, Mark, but how do I protect my son from what they're so obviously capable of?'

The anguish in her voice had him pulling her closer and into his arms, hoping to provide the warmth, comfort and reassurance she needed. Instead, it stirred feelings in him he had no right to feel when her life — and her son's — were in danger. He cuddled her closer as her arms wrapped around his waist and she rested her head against his chest. Gently he stroked her hair before placing a kiss on the top of her head. *Becoming a habit*, his conscience chastised but he ignored the warning.

He had no idea how long they stood like that, bathed in the moonlight, looking out over the peaceful valley, her head nestled against his heart and his arms holding her there.

Lily wasn't complaining. The steady beat of his heart promised more than sanctuary. It promised hope, security and fulfilment. It promised the answers and closure which she and Luke needed to be able to move on from their past, to rebuild their future and live with the freedom they deserved.

She hugged Mark a little tighter. It felt so damn good to be held, comforted, *safe*. Once again doubt niggled at her mind. Was this tingling desire she felt for him real? Or was it transference because he'd rescued her, championed their case, promised to remove the threat that hung over their heads like a bucket of cold water balanced on the top of a door?

'You're thinking too much, Lily.' His voice rumbled against her cheek. The flat of his hand stroked a soothing circular path against her back until she relaxed once more.

Lily lifted her face to his. 'I know. I wish it was over.'

'So do I, honey, so do I.'

The finger under her chin was warm as he tilted her face up further. The warmth of his eyes kissed her lips, and she parted them to take an expectant breath. Mesmerised, she watched as his head descended, blocking out the moonlight. Her lips met his with a gentle eagerness and she felt the firm rub of his mouth across hers. Warm and delicious, she enjoyed the pressure he made no move to deepen ... just enjoy.

Her hands found their way inside his shirt and up the heated skin of his back. Firm muscles rippled under her exploration, and she felt him grow hard against her. His own hands wandered into the curve of her spine, stroked the firmness of her hips through the rough denim of her jeans. Still his lips only tempted hers.

'Where's that bloody Mark got to?' Harold's voice boomed out through the kitchen door.

'Mind your own bloody beeswax,' Lily heard Olive reply.

With a sigh, Mark lifted his head. 'When this is over ...'

Lily smiled up at him and moved out of his arms. 'Yes, when this is over.' On feet that felt a little unsteady, she walked over to a deck chair and sat just as Harold stepped out onto the veranda.

'Come on, pretty boy. Time to go. Olive says you need your beauty sleep, and she wants you to take her home.'

'Harold Jones, don't you go telling porky pies!' Olive's cane tapped against the kitchen floor.

Lily rose from the chair. 'Let's go inside then. I'd hate for you to lose any beauty sleep, Mark.' She led the way into the kitchen, relaxed, happy and just a little frustrated.

Annoyed, irritated, frustrated from a night of tossing and turning, filled with dreams of Lily, followed by a cold shower, Mark was in no mood for fun and games. He attacked the whiteboard in his office with a vengeance until it resembled a rainbow of boxes and connecting arrows, and he'd run out of colours.

He'd worked through the evidence he'd retrieved from the cold case store, shuddered as he'd gone through it, remembering the danger his sister and her daughter had faced. He'd found payments, transfers and linked them to a business account — Albero and Bennetti's Law firm — surprise, surprise. Tiny's drawings began to make sense. He'd drawn a reverse hierarchy. Each sketch on the bricks of his graffiti wall resembled a package drop and there, to the left of the intertwined snakes, was a stick person leaning on a dollar sign holding a golden statue, a speech bubble with the words *I paid the Price*.

Harold whistled through his teeth as he stepped into the room, a takeaway coffee in each hand. 'Fuck me, you've been busy. Here, I brought you real coffee to make up for the donkey pee we had to drink earlier.'

'Not only busy, but I found the link to Price.'

'Why am I not surprised,' mumbled Harold. 'Go on, tell me.'

'First things first. Did you get a look at that USB that was in the box of stuff Lily found?'

'Yep. They appear to be recordings, like a voice recorder on a mobile phone, very sketchy quality. The techs have copied it and I'm waiting for them to iron out the distortion and load it up with their fancy voice recognition software.'

'Good work. All we need is something concrete enough to bring Albero in with a warrant. I don't want him wriggling.' Mark rubbed at the headache forming between his brows. He took a coffee from Harold. 'Let's listen to those recordings over coffee.'

His partner shrugged. 'Got nothing better to do.'

Mark inserted the USB into a port on his laptop and scanned the files. Dates not names, he figured looking at the file names. 'I guess we'll start with the first one then.' He double-clicked on the file and waited for the media file to load. Cold fingers crept up his spine as he listened to recording after recording and prayed the evidence would hold up in court.

Lily looked around her office with a smile. *Her* office — another step closer to freedom, to independence, yet another positive move forward out of the darkness that ruled their past. She placed a potted, double-flowered begonia on the sunny windowsill and arranged the items on her desk.

'Settling in okay?' TJ popped her head around the door.

'Yes, thanks. I'm even getting used to the aroma of "grease 'n shit" everyone seems to wear around here.' She grinned at TJ and pointed to a pile of paperwork on the corner of her desk. 'Where would you like me to start?'

Her first day as Program Coordinator for the Apprenticeship Rehabilitation Program at M&M Motors. As Scott had driven the five of them to work this morning, packed into his four-wheel drive, Lily had sat squished between Marty and Luke, excitement and anticipation fluttering in her stomach.

'I've left you the information file to familiarise yourself with the program procedures and participants. Why not start with that and perhaps you can write down a few ideas for an action plan for each of our apprentices?' TJ dabbed at her hands with an oily rag. 'I'll pop in later to see how you're doing.'

'Thanks, TJ. I really appreciate this.'

TJ smiled. 'No need to thank me. You've saved me hours of interviewing to find the right person for the job. I have complete faith in you.'

Warmth flooded Lily at the comfort of those simple words. *I have complete faith in you.* She hugged those words to her heart as she sat to read through the file. Two hours and several pages of notes later, the phone on her desk rang ... the first official phone call in her newly employed capacity. With a sense of satisfaction, she picked up.

'Good morning, M&M Motors, Lily speaking,' she answered. The chuckle that slithered down the line had unpleasant chills rising up from her stomach to the top of her head. Her icy fingers coiled into the phone cord.

'Well, look at you. Gainfully employed, living the dream with potted plants and a corner office. So naïve, Liliana.'

'What do you want, Nic?'

He was right. She'd been lulled into a false sense of security by the promise of protection, pushed the threat to the back of her mind, too focused on the comfort of here and now. Lily turned in her chair to look out the window. Across the road from the dealership, she spotted a black sedan parked outside the second-hand charity shop. The window rolled down and Albero waved nonchalantly.

'Your detective paid me a visit. You gave them your phones. That was a stupid move. Do you think I don't know all the evidence they have is circumstantial at best? I'm a criminal lawyer, Liliana. I know *all* the loopholes.'

Lily said nothing. What could she say? In her mind, she heard the sound of her dreams of freedom come crashing to earth.

'Nothing to say, Princess? Call the dogs off. Tell them you made a mistake. Luke's scribbles are nothing more than the ramblings of a drug addict, a disturbed teenager ... a *murderer*.'

His words sliced through her with the force of a butcher's knife. Fear cramped her stomach, anger clogged her throat and the grip of her fingers on the phone cord threatened to cut off the circulation in her hands. *Fight or flight?* The thought raced through her mind.

'Give up. You and Luke are loose ends. No-one likes loose ends. Business is suffering from all the attention. Snow gets a little ... trigger-happy when that happens. The two of you disappear, a little family tragedy, a confession ... and all this goes back onto the cold case shelf. It's my job to make these things go away, Liliana. Which would you prefer? Luke in prison at the mercy of his cellmates, afraid to bend over in the shower? You living in fear, looking over your shoulder, wondering when it will be your turn? I'm offering you the easy way out. Your life is worthless, no matter how much you try to turn it around.'

Lily watched through the window as he opened the car door and stepped out. Immaculately groomed as always, dark hair slicked back, black pin-striped suit pressed, shoes polished until they reflected the rays of the sun, Albero tipped his Ray Bans on his nose to stare at her over them. With a little wave he said, 'You are worthless, Liliana. No-one will miss a grieving widow and a murderous teenager. Somewhere, sometime, you're going to be alone in that garden up in the hills ... and I'll be waiting.'

The line went dead as Lily watched Albero get into his car, ease into the traffic and drive away. It would *never* be over.

Chapter Twelve

s Mark considered the evidence and the action plan he and Harold had put together, his thoughts turned to Lily. How was she enjoying her new job? He'd enjoyed watching a more confident, happier Lily emerge in the week they'd been at the refuge. His fragile angel had more courage than she'd bargained for.

No, he couldn't afford to think of her as his, not until all this was over. The evidence lay spread out over the long table in the conference room at Police Headquarters. A puzzle they'd pieced together enough of to be able to issue a warrant for Albero's arrest. Not for murder but for fraud, enough for a start, enough to request DNA testing — evidence that would hopefully lead to a confession. A result that would tie Albero in so many knots he wouldn't have a loophole to wriggle through.

Mark picked up his phone off the table. He needed to hear her voice, to know she was safe. As the net began to tighten around them, Albero and Snow would get jumpy, careless. He needed to make sure Lily and Luke were out of their reach. His gut churned at the thought of what the thugs were capable of.

The need to call her grew stronger and he dialled the number of the mobile TJ had given her to use. It rang until it cut out. The uneasiness in his gut churned in his throat. He dialled the number at M&M Motors and got through to the receptionist.

'May I speak with Lily Bennetti, please?'

'One moment, I'll put you through.'

He waited, his instincts already in over-drive, the keys for his car in his hand.

'I'm sorry, but Lily is not at her desk at the moment. May I take a message for her?'

The force with which his heart met his stomach made him dizzy as he leaned on the table. He fought against his instincts. Perhaps she was having lunch, following up on a query, doing something. 'Put me through to TJ Devin.'

Harold entered the room, but Mark couldn't lift his head to acknowledge him. A headache began to pound at his temples. If Albero had done something to Lily ...

'Hello, workshop.'

TJ's cheery voice didn't soothe his nerves, not this time. 'TJ, where's Lily and Luke?'

'Hello to you too, Detective Johnson. I'm fine thank you. How are you? Last time I saw them they were having lunch. I try not to make them slave through their breaks. It's against the law.'

'TJ, the shit is about to hit the fan and I have a funny feeling. Can you find Lily for me?'

'I know better than to argue with your gut.' Mark heard voices, doors opening and closing, the rhythm of TJ's breathing in his ear as she walked through the dealership. With every step she took, his heart pounded a little harder and the ache in his stomach grew. 'Steve! Have you seen Lily or Luke?' He heard her call, not even wincing as she yelled in his ear. Steve's response was a muffled negative. TJ moved again. 'Aah ... *shit*.'

Mark's heart plummeted further. 'What is it, TJ?' But in the depths of his soul, he knew what his instinct had been telling him all morning.

'Get your arse down here, Detective. Lily's gone.'

Lily turned the car into the station parking lot. With guilt dragging on her shoulders, she pulled out the envelope of money she'd taken from the office safe. There was enough there for the train tickets, accommodation for a week or so, and to buy food.

Somehow she would find a way to pay the money back. As long as Albero didn't find her and Luke. Where they would head to she had no idea, but the Nullarbor was long. There were plenty of stops along the way. Somewhere obscure, where no-one knew them. Maybe they could get off at Cook in the middle of the Nullarbor Plain. The ghost town — population two, sometimes three if you counted the driver swap — had to have somewhere they could hide for a while. Or maybe Kalgoorlie—a little bigger but still obscure.

'You got your bag, Luke?'

'Yeah.'

She'd pick up a few packets of nibbles and bottled water at the station shop. That would at least keep them going until they reached Kalgoorlie. She typed a text to TJ, then placed the phone in the glove box. Grabbing her bag from behind her seat, she sat a moment, regret pooling in her belly.

'I'm sorry, Luke. It's the only way I know how to get us out of this mess.'

'Sure.'

'I have to keep us alive.'

'Yep.'

'A life on the run. Hopefully, Mark will solve the case and we can get our lives back.' She zipped up her bag and squeezed his hand where he clutched his backpack.

'What about my bail, Mum? I'll go to juvie for sure.

The judge won't be so kind if I break my bail conditions.'

Lily swallowed past the fear that gripped her throat. Either way they were in danger, with or without the protection of the justice system. The way she saw it she had no choice but to get them far away from Nic Albero, and fast. 'We'll work something out, Luke. I need time to think it through. Once we're safely away, I'll contact TJ and see what we can do.' She opened the car door. 'For now, let's get going. The train leaves in ten minutes. We can't afford to miss it.'

They got out and Lily locked the car. Using the parcel tape, she'd put in her bag before leaving the dealership, she taped the key to the inside of the wheel arch. A quick look around confirmed there was no sign of Albero's black sedan. She'd been careful to make sure Albero hadn't followed them. With her hand on Luke's arm, Lily took another step into the unknown and yet again, shaky future.

Mark stood at Lily's desk holding the letter she'd left on her notepad. Her neat handwriting quivered in places, and he wondered if it was fear or haste that caused it.

Dearest TJ,

I can't begin to apologise enough. I hope you'll understand. We had to go. I swear I'll pay the money back as soon as I can. Luke and I can't go on looking over our shoulders, waiting for Albero to strike. He's too clever and knows too much about the law. There will be no justice for Luke, or for me. I know everyone is doing their best to help us, but while Albero is free, we will always be in danger. You don't deserve to be in the same position. Thank you for everything. I wish things could have turned out differently. I'm sorry. Lily and Luke.

He wasn't sure what hurt most. That she hadn't trusted him to keep them safe or that she hadn't come to him before running. He put the letter down on the desk and moved to the window to stroke the leaves of the begonia she'd put there. If he breathed deeply enough, he could smell her perfume in the air. His gut churned at the thought of her — of them — out there, alone and at the mercy of Albero without his protection.

'She's scared, Mark.' Harold's comment did little to soothe him. 'When victims are scared, they run. It's instinct.'

'Instinct, my arse! *God damn it*, Harold. Why didn't she come to us first?' He bagged the letter irritably. It sucked. Big time. Like a kick in the balls.

'Stop thinking with your dick and think like a cop. This arsehole lawyer killed a kid, blew up her house, threatened more than once to kill her and her son. Her husband was a drug-dealing bastard who got his own son involved in his crap and defended the people in court who put the damn stuff on the streets. How much faith do you think she has in the law right now?'

As every word Harold said hit home, arrowing through his heart, he knew his partner was right, but still ... he loved her. She should have come to him. Mark swept an irritable hand through his hair. What a perfectly shit time to realise you were in love with a woman so far out of reach, it made Mars look like a liveable option.

TJ stepped into the office. 'I've got a text from Lily.' She handed her phone to Mark.

Car @ Sth Perth Stn. Keys under RF arch. Phone in glove box. Sorry. L

'I'll send a couple of the boys to pick it up. If the police, tow truck or I go it might attract Albero's attention,' TJ said. 'When it's back here, you can go through it. It's not like it's a murder investigation, is it? There's no evidence to contaminate.'

Harold nodded. 'Agreed. Did Lily say anything to you about Albero contacting her again?'

TJ shook her head. 'Not a word. She was so excited about getting started on the program coordination. Look at the progress she'd made.' She waved a hand at the notes Lily had made and the file, now a rainbow of Post-it notes. 'He must have called her earlier today.'

'I'll have a chat with the receptionist. See if she remembers anything,' Harold said, moving toward the door. 'Are you coming?'

Mark shook his head. 'I'll look through her desk. See if she left anything else behind. How much money did she take, TJ?'

TJ shrugged. 'I'll have to count it.' She stepped over to the safe, punched in the combination and waited for the click of the locks. The door released and she opened it. 'Wasn't much. There's not much of a dent. A couple of thousand, I guess?'

How far could two people go on a couple of thousand dollars, he wondered. Not very far. With a sigh, he opened the drawers under her desk and found nothing except stationery. He tapped the mouse to wake her computer. Google ... but the browsing history had been cleared. Forensics could deal with that when the time came.

Harold came into the office. 'Receptionist remembers a call coming through for Lily from a man at around 11:30 a.m. Doesn't prove anything. Could've been an enquiry about the program.'

Mark sighed. 'We need something more concrete.'

'Guess I'll be looking into Albero's phone records again?'

'That's about all we have to go on at the moment,' Mark replied. 'I think it's time to bring him in. Screw it. We have enough on him to start questioning him.'

'Don't rush it. There's still the little matter of Serena Snow. Wherever Lily is, she's safe for now. As long as Albero doesn't know she's missing. We have to keep that very quiet until we can arrange the warrant. We don't want him disappearing too.'

'How long?' Mark struggled to keep the impatience from his voice.

'A day to subpoena his phone records — again, plus time to present the evidence to obtain the warrant ... I'd say a couple of days at best. He won't push his luck by trying to contact her again too quickly. He'll wait, let her stew and then prod her again. He knows how to play the game.'

'Bastard thinks he can hide behind his law degree. I can't wait to throw his arse in prison.'

Harold thumped Mark's shoulder. 'When we do, I promise to turn my back so you can beat the crap out of him. Only if you promise to do the same for me. But right now, buddy, let's get this show on the road, so we can find your damsel in distress, and you can scratch that bloody itch that's putting that soppy look in your eyes.'

Chapter Thirteen

The wheels of the Indian Pacific rolled along the tracks with a soothing rhythm as the train devoured the distance on its ten-hour journey to Kalgoorlie. Lily had no idea where they would get off the train. She'd paid for tickets all the way to Sydney. It would be easy to disappear there. Sydneysiders were too busy to ask questions. Anonymity ... it was exactly what they needed to get their feet under them.

With Luke asleep beside her, she welcomed the quiet of the evening that hung in their double cabin, the cheapest travel she could get at such short notice.

By now, TJ would have called Mark to let him know they were missing. What was he thinking? He would be angry with her for sure. Rightly so. Perhaps, she should have trusted him to protect her. Would it have made a difference? The wheels of justice turned far too slowly and really, what chance did they have of nailing Albero down. He was a lawyer and, as he'd pointed out, he knew the loopholes ... too well.

For a single moment, she'd thought about calling Mark, seeking the comfort of his voice, perhaps even the warmth of his arms. But her dependence on a man had got her into trouble before. Not that Mark was anything like Gino, it was simply too soon. The years of abuse, physical and mental destroyed trust and dreams of happy ever afters. Dreaming of a life with Mark was far too dangerous. He had as much power over her as Albero did, as Gino had once had. She craved freedom and independence, if only for a little while.

Mark held their future in his hands. If he couldn't prove Nic Albero and Serena Snow guilty and put them both away, her life and Luke's were worthless. They were as good as dead. Nothing had changed.

Still, she longed to hear his voice. Hear him tell her it would be okay. Hold her against him one more time, so she could feel his strength, hear the beat of his heart beneath her ear.

She should have kept the phone. No, that would give him a trace on them. It was just her and Luke. It had to be that way for however long it took to prove Luke wasn't a murderer. He was simply an innocent child caught up in the dark tunnels of the underworld, put there by the man who'd fathered him.

She would never understand what had driven Gino

to do that to their son, the boy who now slept next to her on the train with his lashes touching his cheeks. If he'd told Gino no, would they be here right now? The word "no" meant nothing to Gino. It never had. Her body and mind bore the scars to testify to it, as did Luke's.

Lily watched the black of night flash by the carriage window, dotted with the occasional blitz of light from the train signals along the way. As they thundered on toward Kalgoorlie, Lily thought her life as endless and barren as the Nullarbor.

'Look what arrived in the internal mail.' Harold waved two envelopes in the air, one in each hand.

Mark rubbed tired eyes and pushed back the reports on his desk. At eleven o'clock at night and after the turmoil of the day, he was grumpy and dying for a decent coffee. 'About fucking time,' he grumbled.

Harold smacked him on the back of the head with the envelopes. 'Fancy a trip to Albero's place?'

'No, but I'd fancy a trip to his fucking funeral.'

'Well, aren't you just a bundle of joy today. I'm guessing there's still no word from Lily?'

'Ten hours, Harold. Ten lousy, *fucking* hours. They could be anywhere by now. How can I be sure Albero hasn't tracked them down already?'

'Because the arsehole only left his office to go home a couple of hours ago.'

'Doesn't mean he doesn't have people to do his dirty work. Like my ex-brother-in-law or the thugs he employed.'

Harold smirked as he smoothed out the warrant for Albero's arrest. 'They arrived in Kalgoorlie at 10:20 p.m. on the Indian Pacific.'

'*What?*'

Harold shrugged, nonchalant. 'Lily and Luke. They arrived by train in Kalgoorlie a little over half an hour ago.'

'How the fuck do you know that?' Mark stood, shooting out a hand to grab his mug before it spilt cold coffee all over his paperwork. 'Weren't you the one who told me *not* to start a missing persons search?'

'Yes, because *you* need to concentrate on getting this case wrapped up. While you were wallowing in self-pity and red tape, I did a little digging. The car was at the South Perth train station, right? That line goes to Sydney. The ticket office recalls asking for a delay in departure so two latecomers could board — with one-way tickets. The conductor on the Indian Pacific remembers a pretty blonde and her son getting off the train in Kal. He wondered why when their tickets were booked all the way to Sydney. Apparently, she's wearing that same lost look as you are. All they had with them was hand luggage according to the conductor.'

Mark sank into his chair, relief flooding through him. Thank God. They were safe. For now, at least. 'Problem is, if you found them that easily, Albero could too. We need to move on this fast.'

'I'll let the local cops know.'

'Have I told you lately you're not such a dickhead after all, Harold? Better not get too soft or you'll be watching those chick flicks with Jeannie and Olive before you know it.'

Harold snorted. 'Too late. They hide the remote and I'm forced to.'

Mark smiled a little. 'There are so many things I could say to that but right now all I want to do is slap the chains on Nic Albero. Preferably around his grungy neck so I can hang him from the shower head in prison like the fly bait he is. Let's visit Mr Albero and show him his room for the night.'

'Now you're talking my language! No more of this soppy crap. Next thing I know you'll be hopping on a plane to Kalgoorlie with a bunch of roses and a proposal.'

'Bullshit. And don't tell me you never gave Jeannie flowers.' Mark snatched up his keys. 'Let's go.'

Silence stretched between them as they drove. All Mark wanted was for it to be over. When they pulled up outside Albero's house ten minutes later, he was determined it would be. Lily and Luke would be free then, free to live their new life. Would Lily decide to stay away from Perth? Start afresh on the east coast, or somewhere else? He forced down the ache of emptiness that settled around his heart. It had to be her choice.

With a shrug, he squared his shoulders, patted the pocket bulging with the envelope containing the warrant and took a deep breath. He let it out on a sigh. 'Ready when you are, partner.'

They got out of the car and made their way up to Albero's front door. The path lit up like a cricket pitch at a night game as motion sensor security lights snapped on.

Harold whistled. 'Anyone would think our big bad lawyer is scared of the dark.'

'More like what will come out of the shadows to bite his arse. I think you need one of those fountains in your front yard.' Mark pointed to the centre of the circular driveway.

'Fuck off! Bloody naked ladies, seriously? And is that a giant ... no, surely not!' Harold shook his head at the hedge clipped in a long, fat rounded sculpture with a bulbous shape at the top of it. 'A dick for dick — figures. He has some seriously shitty taste, this bloke.'

Mark chuckled as he pressed the doorbell, ringing it until Albero whipped the door open. He waved the warrant under Albero's nose. 'I'm sure you're familiar with this?' He made to push past Albero, who blocked his way in.

'What the fuck? Do you know what fucking time it

is? You can't force your way into my house! Who the fuck do you think you are? This is fucking harassment!' Anger reddened his face, the cords of his neck rigid with fury.

'Nice PJs,' said Harold, pointing to Albero's silk robe. 'Who dresses you? Your mother?'

Mark showed him the warrant again. 'We have a few questions to ask you.'

'I have nothing to tell you.'

'Really?' Taking his time, Mark opened the envelope and pulled out two pieces of paper. 'You see, Albero, I have something here I think might interest you.'

'I'm not interested in anything you have to show me, Detective. Get off my property.'

'Or what? We have a warrant that says we can be here. If I was you, I'd pay attention,' Harold interjected.

'Well, you're not me, arsehole. I don't know what you *think* you have on me, but I'll find a loophole and I'll drag your sorry arses through the courts until they strip you of everything you've worked for.'

'You know when you sneer like that you look like an ugly Pitbull? Slobber like one too.' Harold flicked at the sleeve of his shirt.

'Shall we sit and talk about this like real men?' Mark said affably, as Albero's glance fell on the government logo on the paper he held. 'You'll want to see this.'

'Who is it, Babe?' Albero's secretary appeared in the doorway, rumpled and wearing a robe matching his.

'No-one. Go to bed, Bitch.'

Harold raised an eyebrow. 'That's your sexy talk? I can see it really turns them on,' he said as the girl's eyes teared up and she walked away with a sniff.

'Get on with it and get out. I'm tired.'

'I bet you are,' Harold said, earning himself another derogatory look.

Mark smiled. 'Tell me, Nic, had you ever met Tiny Watts before he started running drugs for you and Serena Snow?'

'I have no idea what you're talking about. Like you, Detective Johnson, I'm an officer of the law.' He ignored Harold's snort of disgust. 'I've told you I only know Tiny Watts through Luke Bennetti. He and Luke were mates.'

'You might want to invite us in, Nicky my boy,' said Harold. 'You're going to need a chair.'

'I don't let pigs in my house. They make a mess of the place.'

'I bet they do with all the shit you're hiding.' Harold leaned against the wall next to the front door, a foot on the curved step.

'I've got nothing to hide.'

Mark unfolded the paper in his hand and studied it. 'Well, that's interesting. Are you sure about that? Do you have any children, Nic?'

Albero smirked. 'No. I managed to avoid that trap.'

Harold and Mark looked at each other with a grin that made Albero shuffle his feet. 'What's your point?'

'Well, you see, we have evidence that points to you and Bennetti being at the convention centre around the time Tiny Watts disappeared. We have a witness who saw you in the park near the toilets where he was murdered.' Mark studied the nervous flicker of Albero's eyes, the twitch of the muscle in his face.

'Bullshit. I've already told you I didn't know the kid.'

'But you did know he was a foster child?'

'What has that got to do with anything? The kid was a loser, a drug addict, a fucking troublemaker!' Albero leaned a shoulder against the doorframe, his lips drawn in a smug smile. 'You're wasting your time, Detective, and taxpayer dollars.'

Mark's hands itched to punch the arrogance from his puffy face. He stroked a hand over the paper instead, a far more powerful weapon. 'I disagree, Nic. You see, according to this little piece of paper ...' He placed it against the wall and smoothed it down, '... you murdered your own son.'

White-faced and sweating, Albero held out his hand for the paper. Mark handed it over without a word. Expressions chased across the lawyer's face as he took in dates, places and the names on Tiny Watts's birth certificate. '*Jesus ...*'

'Now that's not exactly what I'd call you,' said Mark.

~

Kalgoorlie, the city of gold. Lily scanned the rows of heritage buildings, taking in the dull, aging facades and the dry and dusty land on which they stood. If the streets were truly lined with gold here, why didn't she feel lucky? Something in her bones — a nagging feeling — had her hesitating, wondering if this was far enough away. A nice town but not nearly remote enough, too busy, Lily thought.

The train had stopped for fuel and to stock up on supplies, leaving them twenty minutes to stretch their legs. It was tempting not to board the train again, but Broken Hill looked far more promising. Lily's heart lifted a little only to plunge again as she thought of Luke and how with every long kilometre of their journey, he'd retreated more.

Bugger it. She was tired of running from Gino's ghost. Kalgoorlie it was. Anyone looking for them would think they'd gone all the way to Sydney. Neither she nor Luke could take much more.

'We're not getting back on the train, Luke.'

'*What?*'

She'd had time to think but still found no comfort in

doing the right thing and going to the local police to explain their situation and tell them about Luke's bail conditions. Sure, the cops would contact Mark, let him know they were okay and where they were. No, it wouldn't work. They could end up being extradited back to Perth. The longer she left it, the worse the consequences could be for Luke. She missed TJ, her garden, even her little cabin ... and Mark. Good memories best let go. At least until Albero no longer posed a threat. If justice served. So far it hadn't.

Luke had retreated into the sullen boy he'd been before Gino's death. It hurt. She was losing him ... again. Guilt flooded through her once more. What a mess she'd made of her son's life. No wonder he hadn't spoken more than two words to her since leaving Perth. Tears stung her eyes as pain constricted her throat. Here they were, in the middle of nowhere, on their way to who-knew-where with an uncertain future keeping pace behind them.

'What's the point? We can't keep running forever. I'm sorry, Luke,' she whispered, cringing as he pulled his hoodie up over his head and turned away from her.

Behind them the train whistle blew, and the brakes screamed as they released, letting the wheels turn freely. Vaguely she heard a scuffle, a shout from the conductor but she paid no attention. Her eyes were on Luke. She stared at his thin shoulders hunched away from her against the harsh light of the station platform and felt the wall of silence grow. Their hopes, their dreams and their future happiness slammed into that wall and shattered, the shards piercing her heart. Perhaps they were better off dead.

Chapter Fourteen

The last time he'd stepped into interview room one, he'd seen an angel. Now all Mark saw was the devil, and at one o'clock in the morning, his patience had run out. Nic Albero hadn't come quietly, and he showed no signs of talking. If Mark wanted to bring Lily home — and *oh God*, he wanted to — he had to get a full confession out of Albero. All he needed was something concrete — anything — that pointed to Serena Snow, and he'd have them both.

Tonight was surely the longest night of his life. What was Lily doing? Were they okay? They were safe for now and that's all that mattered to him, all he could afford to think of until this was over. Now all Mark wanted was to wrap up this case and put the boxes back in the archives. The best way to keep Lily and Luke safe and give them back their freedom, was to put his time and skills to the best use he could.

'Tell me about the Golden Diva.'

'Fuck you.'

Mark put a restraining hand on Harold's arm as he pushed back his chair, ready to grab Albero around the neck. As much as he wanted to strangle the arrogant bastard himself, he didn't want to give Albero any room to wriggle out of the corner they'd put him in.

'Answer the question. If you're looking to plea bargain, it will count in your favour,' Mark reminded him.

'Don't tell me the law. I don't have to answer your question. I know my rights.'

Mark sighed. His long night looked like it was going to get even longer. 'I have enough on your petty crimes to throw your sorry arse in prison until your preliminary hearing at least. Don't make it harder than it needs to be.'

'Fine, I'll make it personal instead. Your ex-brother-in-law, Paul Price, sold us shares to buy himself out of the debt he owed.'

'Who's *we*?' Mark's fingers hurt from clenching them in a fist, holding the punch he'd love to deliver to Albero's chin. For his sister, for his niece, even for Luke. But most of all, for Lily.

'Myself, Gino and Serena Snow.'

'How do you know Serena Snow?'

'Not that it's any of your business but we met years ago, had a thing going for a while. What's this got to do with anything anyway? Are you charging me for having a relationship?' Albero reclined in the chair and linked his hands across his fat belly.

'Did you know she was pregnant?'

'That bitch opened her legs for anything with a dick. Yes, I knew. I told her to have an abortion. I would have paid for it even though there was no proof the bastard was mine. That birth certificate you have is a lie.' He smoothed the silk of his robe. 'You pricks could have let me put pants on.'

'Why did you murder Tiny Watts?' Mark leaned forward on his elbows and held Albero's gaze.

Albero took a while to respond, and Mark wondered what was going through his mind. 'You have nothing, Detective. Now you're reaching.'

'Do you think she knew Tiny Watts was her son?'

Albero stared at him, his eyes cold, the muscle in his cheek twitching. 'There was no child.'

Mark pulled out a copy of the maternity hospital records they'd subpoenaed after finding Tiny's stash. 'This says there was.' He handed the paper to Albero. 'The blood type is the same as yours and I bet if we did DNA tests it would come up with a match. You murdered your son. He died an excruciating death by your hand with your drugs. That makes you a monster.'

Albero shrugged but said nothing. Pasty white

replaced the ruddiness on his puffy cheeks, the smug look and self-assurance wearing off. The cracks had started to show.

'How did Tiny end up a runner for her?'

Albero remained silent. Harold stood to walk the length of the room and back as they waited for a response. When their suspect leaned forward on the table but still stayed tight-lipped, he stopped pacing and said, 'You know, Nic, I've a mind to send you to maximum security until we can book that prelim. It wouldn't be too hard to arrange.' He strolled around the table to stand behind Albero. 'The prison guards will talk, the inmates will listen and by dinner time, you'll be someone's bitch.'

'Fuck you.'

Harold chuckled. 'No, fuck *you*. Because when your cellmate is done with you, he'll pass you around for the others to play with and — from what I hear — they don't much like your kind in there. The clean-up crew will be scraping what's left of you from the walls and floor of the showers.'

Mark leaned back in his chair. 'You know all about that, don't you? How many of those little *meetings* have you arranged on visits to your clients?' He drew gallows and a noose on his notepad. 'My guess is there are a few people in there looking for payback. The morgue has seen a few of your mates on the slab recently. I wonder if your number will be up next?' With a few strokes of the pen, he drew a stickman with his head through the noose. 'Game over.'

'I want a lawyer.'

'You *are* a lawyer. Do yourself a favour and run your own defence. Everyone else out there in the legal world would be happy to see you rot in prison.'

'Then I want solitary confinement until the trial.'

Mark raised his eyebrows. 'Afraid they'll rip you a new arsehole? I'm not sure you're in a position to bargain yet. Give me something to work with.'

'Serena hung out at the train stations, watched for the troublemakers, the homeless kids — kids who weren't likely to be missed if anything happened to them.' Albero wiped his mouth and stubbly chin with the flat of his hand.

'Irony is an ugly mistress,' Mark said. 'Where is she?'

'I don't know.'

'You're lying. Who else is involved?'

'What do I get in exchange?'

Albero's smirk stretched Mark's self-control as he gripped the pen in his hand. Mark narrowed his eyes. 'Tell me where Serena Snow is, and we'll talk.'

Albero leaned back in the interview chair, his eyes emotionless. 'Worried about the lovely Liliana, Detective? That cold bitch and her snivelling boy deserve everything coming their way.'

'Answer the question, you dickhead,' Harold

intervened. 'Your own bedroom in the lock up isn't looking like a deal right now.'

Mark studied Albero's face as he leaned toward him over the table between them. The man's features were set like stone. Not so much as a muscle twitched as he stared at his cuffed hands, his lips pulled tight. 'Why did you threaten to kill Lily and Luke?' Mark asked.

Albero's lips stretched. 'Serena wanted them gone after Luke shot Gino.'

'So, you would murder another *child* and an innocent woman to appease her?' Mark shook his head. 'What about Scott Devin?'

Albero played with the chain between his cuffed hands and snorted. 'What about him? He was simply another chess piece in the game, a sucker who fell for what Serena offered, another way to get rid of dirty cash.'

'He's not as much of a sucker as you think. He saw through her game pretty quickly. Greed breeds mistakes, Nic. Deadly mistakes. How does it feel knowing you're just another pawn in a *woman's* game of power?' Mark pushed his chair back and stood. 'You're nothing but Serena Snow's lap dog. You stood by and watched while your partner physically abused his wife and child, deliberately put them in danger. You dealt drugs to children, knowing it would destroy their lives. Then you held down your own *son* and delivered a dose you *knew* would kill him. How does that make you feel?'

Albero lifted his head and held Mark's gaze. 'He was *not* my son,' he bit out through clamped teeth.

'He was *someone's* son, Nic. Would *knowing* he was your son have made a difference? Would *knowing* Luke was Gino's son have stopped you from murdering him too if Snow gave the word? You blew up Lily Bennetti's house *knowing* they'd be going home that day, *knowing* they'd be in the house when the gas ignited.' Mark's chair fell with a crash as he pounded a fist on the table in front of Albero. The cords in his neck stood proud as he battled to keep a rein on his temper. His fists itched to smash into Albero's jaw. 'You're a heartless murderer, Mr Albero. I'm going to ask you one more time. Where is Serena Snow?'

'You think you're so smart, don't you, Detective Johnson,' Albero sneered. 'If you were really that smart, you would have checked the Indian Pacific's passenger manifest. You're too late. By now, Liliana and Luke have had a little accident. Trains are dreadful things. People fall off them so easily.'

Knowing Lily and Luke had arrived safely in Kalgoorlie gave Mark some comfort. If Albero was right and Serena Snow was right behind them ... the possibilities had dread crawling down his spine and squeezing his gut. 'You miserable, fucking bastard!' Mark grabbed the front of Albero's shirt in his fists and dragged him up out of the chair. 'You call yourself a lawyer, a keeper of justice? You're about to find out just what justice is.' He shoved him against the wall. 'If Serena Snow has gone after the Bennettis, I'm going to make sure your stay in prison is a very long and unpleasant one.'

'Not if I counter-sue for ill-treating me in custody. You'll be the one in court, Detective. Go on, I know you want to take a swing at me,' Albero taunted. 'I wonder how the chief will feel when it comes out you've been smelling her arse like a dog on heat?'

Mark let him go and turned away. Anger boiled inside him warring with fear for Lily and Luke. Serena Snow wouldn't play nice with them.

He ran a hand through his hair and over his face, drawing the tension and anger along with it. 'Take him away, Harold. I'm sure his buddies are looking forward to a little reunion over at Supermax.'

Behind him, Harold dragged Albero toward the door. In the reflection of the one-way glass on the wall of the interrogation room, Mark saw Nic Albero turn from the door.

'For the record, Detective ... I might have agreed to have my name on that birth certificate but I sure as hell wasn't the only one who could have fathered her bastard. Your ex-brother-in-law dipped his dick in the pond there, and I can guarantee Gino did too — sometimes all three of us at once. I might be the last one to revisit that little pleasure house, hence my name on the birth certificate, but any one of us could have been the father.'

Mark's skin crawled with loathing for this heartless cockroach. He'd like nothing more than to stamp him out like one. It was cases like these when he could appreciate that sometimes the justice served in the dark corners of a maximum-security prison was more effective than the sentence.

The Desert Inn was the perfect place to stay. According to the brochure Lily had picked up at the station, the rates were reasonable, and they offered long or short-term accommodation. Tired and disillusioned, Lily walked ahead up the gravel pathway lit by solar garden lights as Luke trudged glumly behind. The guest house rambled across the dust. Burnt orange walls, lit up against the night, would blend into the landscape in daylight. Lily's eye was drawn to the Aboriginal painting that graced an adjoining arm of the building.

'Come on in,' a friendly voice called over the tinkling of the copper door bell. 'I'm Dawn. Looking for a place to stay? Aah, for two, then?' A lady with bright crimson hair waved a hand at Luke.

'Umm, yes,' replied Lily.

'Do you have a booking, love?'

'No.'

Dawn chuckled, a rough smoky sound. Lily wondered if it was caused by smoking or inhaling the choking red dust for too long. Colourful plastic-framed glasses slipped down on Dawn's nose as she studied Lily carefully. 'Hmmm ... what's your name, love?'

'Lily Ben ... Benjamin.'

The throaty chuckle deepened until it resembled a magpie call. 'Okay, I got ya. I'll put you in a twin room with an ensuite. How long will you be staying?'

'I ... I'm not sure. If I can find work, we'll stay on.'

Dawn considered her for a moment, her kind yet assessing eyes looking deep beyond Lily's nervousness. 'Righto, I'll give you our long-term rate then. It works out cheaper. If you and the young man there can help out in the dining room at breakfast, I can knock another thirty bucks off the price. You know, clear tables, stock up the tea and coffee, that kinda stuff. We're always looking for extra hands.' She reached up to take a key from the hook behind the desk and scribbled a note in the guest register. Apparently the computer age hadn't quite reached The Desert Inn reception desk yet. 'The mining boom has kept us pretty busy the last coupla years.'

Exhausted, grateful and near tears, Lily nodded. 'Thanks.'

Dawn patted her hand. 'You're welcome, love. Go to the end of the building, turn left and the room is first on your right. Number 8, a lucky number you know.' Dawn waved a ringed hand in the right direction and shooed them away.

Lily figured they needed all the luck they could get. They'd need a change of clothes too, she thought, mentally counting her remaining dollars. 'Um ... is there a second-hand clothing store nearby? We ... lost our luggage in Perth.' She hated lying. There'd been far too much of it in their lives already.

'Now that's a shame,' Dawn said, sympathetically. 'There's a Salvos in the city centre. They open at nine in the morning. It's about a two-minute walk from here. Tell them I sent ya. Meanwhile, I'll lend you two a change of clothes out of lost and found. Laundered them myself, so they're nice and fresh.' She shook her head. 'The things people leave behind...'

Relief joined the weariness reaching into her bones, her soul, and her mind. *I wish this was over. The lies, the deception, the running.* 'Thank you,' she said again, the meaning deeper this time.

'No worries, love. Come around this way. I have a cupboard with some clothes in different shapes and sizes for you two to choose from. It will at least see you through tonight and tomorrow. Been meaning to turn them over to the Salvos. Haven't had time, you see.'

Lily selected a pair of jeans and a t-shirt each — not quite their size or style, but they'd do. She thanked Dawn and agreed they'd be in the kitchen to start work at 5:00 a.m. Luke hadn't spoken a word since getting off the train. His responses to her questions or attempts at conversation were restricted to nods or grunts.

She didn't have the heart to reprimand him. They'd taken two steps forward and three steps back. Their future yawned before them dark and empty, uncertainty breeding in the shadows. At least when Gino was alive, she knew what to expect, how to meet it head on and when to avoid it.

Toughen up, Lily! You can do this! If she told Mark where they were, what would he do? Had they arrested Nic Albero yet? Did they have enough to make an arrest? What was Mark thinking? Would he turn against her for running? What would happen to Luke? The questions raced through her mind. If only she had all the answers.

For a moment, she allowed herself to daydream. Somewhere in the future, when all this was over, would Mark take her in those strong arms, hold her against his heart and tell her he loved her? For the first time in her life, she could sink into his embrace, be loved, adored, appreciated and most of all ... safe. She could dream of Luke having a father who cared for him, nurtured him and shared the joys and trials of young adulthood. Mark could be that man. Already, he'd formed a tenuous bond with Luke. If only —

'Mum.' Luke's voice reached into her thoughts as they stopped at the door of their room. 'Will we ever stop running?'

Lily looked at him, pausing as she inserted the key in the door. Gone was the glimpse of the boy he'd been while they'd stayed at the refuge. Life had shown promise there. Luke had even picked up weight, started showing interest in sport, in the outdoors, in ... living. Now the haunted look was back in his eyes and unhappiness dragged his shoulders to a slope.

Lily wished she could find some reassurance for him. *Yes, son, everything will be okay. This dark shadow that rules our lives will lift and we* can *move on from this.* 'I don't know.'

She pushed open the door to yet another strange room. The whiff of stale cigarette smoke she associated with all motels wrinkled her nose. The carpet aged but clean, was a dark muddy brown. Mint green curtains blocked out the dark behind the windows. Nothing at all like their cabin at TJ's place. Lily sighed as exhaustion stole through her. They couldn't hide here forever. There was still the matter of Luke's breach of his bail conditions to deal with, and the only person she could think of talking to about it was Mark.

What would his reaction be? Would he be angry at her for running away? More than likely. The tentative thread of trust between them was broken. Sadness seeped into her bones. Regret tugged at her heart. How was it possible to become so attached to a man in such a short time? Not just the man himself but the integrity, the caring nature and the promise of security he provided. Was that all she wanted? Was the attraction she felt for him simply because he was the complete opposite of Gino?

Lily shook off the thoughts. Now was not the time to be thinking of Mark. She needed to think of Luke. Weariness settled about her shoulders. If only she had the answer to her own questions, she might be able to get them out of this mess. Perhaps she'd feel better in the morning after a good night's rest. She sat on one of the twin beds as Luke closed and locked the door behind him.

'I wish I had the answers, Luke. I've failed you so many times.'

The mattress sagged a little as Luke sat next to her and pushed back his hoodie. 'None of this is your fault, Mum. Gino was a bastard. I could have said no to him, fought back.' Luke studied the room key in his hand. 'But I had to think of you, and the other boys.'

Lily reached for his hand and held it tight. 'I should have left him before you were born. Then none of this would have happened. Tiny would still be alive, and we'd be safe.'

Luke sighed. 'Tiny and Marty, they were street smart but Gino and Nic? They were smarter. If I didn't play along, all three of them would be dead. It was Connor I was most worried about.'

'Why?' Lily let go of his hand, pushed off her shoes and rested against the wall of the room.

Desert heat still radiated off the plasterboard. The candlewick quilt was soft on the bed beneath her hands. It reminded her of her grandma's house, a lifetime ago. Even the smell of the linens — that mixed perfume of laundry powder and mothballs — reminded her of a happier time when her grandma was still alive, and she hadn't met Gino Bennetti yet.

'Connor was the youngest in the gang, right?' She drew her focus back into the motel room time had forgotten.

Luke nodded. 'He's the weakest of all of us. Connor isn't a street kid. His mum raised him alone and he's a pretty decent kid. Every time I told Gino I wanted out, he'd threaten Connor. I couldn't let that happen.'

'Why didn't you come to me, tell me what was going on?'

'Because he said he'd kill you if I did. He was mean, greedy and selfish, Mum. I knew he'd do it.'

'Oh Luke!' Lily scooted away from the wall to sit next to her son. She looped her arm through his and lay her head against his skinny shoulder. 'What an awful mess.' Tears prickled against her lids, her heart aching as she wished she had the power to turn back time.

'Tiny's dead because of me, Mum.' Luke's words fell like stones into the heavy silence between them. He rubbed his thumb into the palm of his hand as he spoke, studying the creases and lines. 'Gino found a list I'd kept of all the places and dates we'd dropped his shipments. I gave it to Tiny to keep. He wanted out after he joined TJ's program, and he needed a little insurance. It fell out of his pocket when Tiny handed over the cash from a delivery and Gino found it on the floor of the clubhouse.'

Lily shivered. She knew the punishment for disobeying Gino. She'd felt it far too many times in her life.

'That's when they went after him at the convention centre. He wouldn't dob me in though,' Luke said. 'He told Gino he'd written them down. I told them it was me, but Snow said Tiny had to die. He was high risk.'

Tears ran down Luke's cheeks and Lily's heart ached for her son. It was easy to hate Gino at that moment. He'd destroyed so many lives with his greed and selfishness.

'I don't want to run any more, Mum. I want to hand myself in.'

'Luke, no!' Lily cried.

'I have to if I want to turn my life around.'

'But Nic's people will get to you in there, Luke. You won't survive the first night and if you do ...' Desperation alternated with fear as she envisioned the life Luke would have in juvie before he could be sent to adult prison when he turned eighteen. It didn't bear thinking about.

'It's the only way we'll stop this, Mum. If you won't phone Detective Johnson, I will.'

Should she call Mark? His number was engraved in her memory. No, not yet. She had to think first. Sleep, that's what they needed. Things might be clearer in the morning.

'Why don't you grab a shower, Luke? I need to think on this a little. I can't let you go to prison.'

'No thinking, no more delaying. I'll go take that shower, but I want you to call him before Nic or Snow catch up with us. We'll be safer in custody. I'd rather we negotiate a deal than live life waiting for them to catch up with us. They will, Mum, and you know that will be the end of it ... of us.' He stood and picked up the pile of clothes Dawn had given him. 'Call him,' he said as he walked into the tiny bathroom and closed the door.

Dear God, how had it come to this? Her child, her baby talked about "cutting deals" and being safer in custody when he should be talking about girls and football. Lily looked at the clock. What was Mark doing now? Was it too late to ask him for help?

Mark signed off on his last report and looked at his watch. Where was Serena Snow now? Albero's taunts might be just that. He knew Lily and Luke had arrived safely in Kalgoorlie but if Snow was on the train and had followed them, who knew what cruel retaliation she was capable of? For what must be the hundredth time, he wished it was over.

Lily had come to mean so much in such a short time. Even Luke had started to warm to him, come out of his shell a little. Mark would have liked the opportunity to show the teen that not all men were ruthless criminals. That being a father meant more than just a name on a birth certificate. A father like his who'd taken him fishing, boating, taught him to drive, introduced him to his first beer, tossed a football. For a brief moment at the refuge, he'd glimpsed the boy Luke had the potential to become. A happy, easy-going young man with a bright future. And Lily ... his brave, beautiful, fragile angel. She felt so right in his arms. That's where he wanted her. When all this was over ...

He glanced at the screen as his phone rang. A private number. He frowned even as his heart skipped a hopeful beat.

'Detective Mark Johnson,' he answered. *Play it cool.*

'Mark, it's Lily.'

All thoughts of remaining detached fled. *Yes!* His heart tripped at the sound of her voice. Keeping his tone neutral was hard. She'd run away, hadn't trusted him enough to stay. Anger blended with relief, enough to put an edge on his tone. 'Lily.' He heard her hesitation, the intake of breath as she felt the sting in the single word.

'I ... I'm sorry. I did what I thought was right.'

'You could have come to me.' He tried to swallow

the hurt in his tone and failed. In his heart he knew, he would never turn his back on Lily.

'My first instinct was to run, to hide and protect Luke. I didn't think I had a choice after everything Nic and Gino have done.'

The teary thickness in her voice, the desperation in her tone, tugged at his heart. 'I promised you I would protect you both. I meant it.'

'I was afraid, Mark ... afraid Albero would get to us before you could. He was there, across the road from M&M, watching me through the window. I don't have much faith in the justice system. It's failed us too many times already.' A touch of anger lit her tone.

There was the fighting spirit, the Lily he knew lay buried deep inside. The woman his heart wanted to set free. Now he had to tell her he'd betrayed her trust anyway by doing what his job demanded he do.

'It's about to fail you again. We had to let the juvenile court know about Luke's disappearance.' The words ripped past the lump in his throat. Silence — empty, echoing silence stretched and yawned. Had she hung up? 'Lily, did you hear what I said? They're going to issue a warrant unless we can persuade them otherwise.' He heard her choke on a sob and his heart softened a little.

'Then do it if you have to!' she shouted down the line, frustration and anger in her voice. 'What was I supposed to do? Sit back and let that bastard Albero threaten us some more? Wait for Serena Snow to show up and make Luke look like a lousy, no-hoper drug addict who'd overdosed? Or the poor helpless widow, so distraught she had to take her own life? Would *that* have made you feel like a *hero*, Detective Johnson?'

Each word pierced his mind, his heart, his soul. A hero? No, what he felt like was an arsehole, but he needed her to reach deep, to prepare for what might happen next if Serena Snow had followed them.

The court battle when it came to it would be bitter and dangerous, digging deep into the underworld of drugs and crime, stirring up more dirt than she'd uncovered before leaving Perth. Keeping it out of the media would be hard. Doing so without losing more lives would be even harder. They had to get to Snow. Yet again, the cop was at war with the man and for the first time in his career, he wasn't sure which one to reach for.

'We have Albero in custody.' Silence stretched once more. All he heard was the sound of her controlling her breathing. The hitch in her voice told him she fought to hold her tears.

'Do you have enough to keep him there?'

'It looks promising.' He sighed, sat back in his chair and rubbed the ache between his eyes. 'I'm sorry, Lily. I wish you'd trusted me enough to come to me first.'

'I'm sure you understand why I couldn't.' A touch of steel echoed in her voice. 'We're in Kalgoorlie.'

'I know. Harold's been asking around.'

'Luke wants to hand himself in.'

Pain stabbed his gut at the hitch in her voice. He'd give anything to hold her in his arms right now, take her home and keep her close. 'I'll make sure he's looked after, Lily ... that you're both taken care of. TJ and Scott are behind you too. We'll fight every step of the way to keep you both safe. I can't promise more than that.'

'I don't want him handing himself in to the local police. They won't know the whole story like you do.'

'They know enough. Albero's little sideline business has quite a reputation out that way. Until now, they haven't had enough to pin anything on him. Where are you staying?'

'At the Desert Inn.'

'Lily, Albero told us Serena Snow followed you onto the train. She did buy a ticket and the conductor remembers her boarding. You and Luke would be safer at the local police station.'

All Mark could hear was the fear in Lily's voice. 'Oh God!'

'It's not safe for you there, honey.' If anything happened to her, he wasn't sure he could live with himself. 'I'll call them to pick you up.'

'No! Luke wants you and only you. He won't trust anyone else, and neither will I.'

Her last words warmed his heart the most, but frustration overrode it. 'Lily, Serena Snow is following you with the intention to kill. She's not dropping in for a cup of tea.'

Ice froze Lily's tone, and he felt the chill all the way down the line. 'I'm well aware of that, Detective Johnson, thank you.'

'I'll be there as soon as I can. Harold is organising a flight, but in the meantime, please, my angel, go to the locals. I want you safe.'

'I can't, Mark. Not without you here. I wouldn't trust them enough not to lock Luke up and then neither of us would have protection. We'll be careful, I promise. If there's any danger, I'll call triple zero.'

'I'll call them, explain it all to them. Just *go*, for God's sake.' He wanted to yell in frustration. Why the hell was Kalgoorlie so damn far away?

'No. She's in no hurry. If she was on the train with us, she had plenty of opportunity to kill us then. If I call the cops now and she's watching, she'll run. I want her put away, Mark, and if that means we stay where she can find us, I'll do it. Just promise me you'll get here as quickly as you can.'

Torn between pride and frustration, Mark clenched his fists on his desk. 'Lock the doors, keep all the windows closed and stay away from them. Don't open up for anybody, for God's sake.' His tone softened. 'She's ruthless, love. The more I study her file, the worse her record gets.'

'I know. Luke's told me. We'll be careful. Hurry, Mark, please.'

Mark closed his eyes, rested his head on the back of his chair and pictured her face in his mind. 'I'll let the court know where you are, so they don't issue a warrant ... and Lily?'

'Yes?'

He paused, unsure whether to say what was on his mind or not. He took the plunge even though he knew it would be the last thing she'd think about right now. 'We need to talk about us. I miss you.'

Annoyance, anger, frustration fizzled as she said, 'I miss you too.'

Chapter Fifteen

'You are a *sook!*' Harold teased, catching the end of the call.

'What are you on about?' Mark shuffled the evidence on the table in front of him.

'You soppy bastard! You told her you missed her. Oh my God, you've got it bad.' He laughed at the flush that crawled up Mark's neck. 'What a *dickwad*!'

Mark looked at the stapler in his hands, tossed it in his palm, weighing up whether to throw it at his partner or not. Instead, he smiled and shrugged. 'I'm a dickwad? What about the time we flew up north to settle that case in Darwin? I seem to remember one of us had to ring home every night to make sure his lady love was safely tucked in bed. It wasn't me!'

'Huh! It was my *honeymoon* that damn case interrupted.'

'You'd already bought the cow, drank the milk,' Mark threw back, pressing a staple into a wad of paper.

'Ha! I'm going to tell Olive you called Jeannie a cow! She'll disinherit you ... after she's whacked you with her cane.'

'Olive loves me.'

'Bloody oath, she does. I've no idea why!' he grumbled, good-naturedly. 'Where are we going with this case, Loverboy?'

'To Hell and back.' Mark grimaced. 'We're going to Kalgoorlie. I need a plane.'

Harold shifted uneasily. 'That makes me nervous. The last time you said that I ended up with a wounded man on board, flying him into the middle of bloody nowhere. He came back engaged, got married and now his wife is pregnant.'

Mark rubbed his chin, feeling the stubble that reminded him he hadn't had time to shave. He hadn't slept either since Lily and Luke's disappearance, and he doubted he would until they were safe. The sooner they got to Kalgoorlie, the sooner he could bring them home to start again. Uncertainty swirled in his stomach. Once Albero and Snow were off the streets, would she still need him? Could her new life include a worn-out detective?

'Well, it won't happen again, will it? You're already taken and too bloody old to have a baby.'

'Yeah, but you're not. Let's hope you still know how

to make babies.' Harold grinned. 'Now, stop moping around and let's get the job done, so you can get some practice in. What's the plan?'

Mark ignored Harold's hint that he and Lily might stand a chance together. It had to be about bringing them home safely first. 'We have Albero's confession and Tiny's evidence. Re-opening the cold case means we can use Price's statements and evidence too. There's video evidence in both cases that shows the three of them together at the Golden Diva. That provides the link in the two cases. Add to that Scott Devin's evidence and the security tapes from the conference centre. Plenty of visuals.' He shuffled the papers around some more. 'A bust catching her red-handed with a shipment would be good, but I don't think we have time for that. With Albero in custody, she'll be getting antsy. She's on her own now. We've taken down her key players.'

'She doesn't know that yet, though. So, we still have the advantage. She might have new playmates lined up already,' suggested Harold.

'God, I hope not. Do we have enough for a search warrant? Where is she staying?'

Harold consulted the file of suspects. 'A rental in South Perth. I can get a team over there for a search in a couple of hours. It's bloody three in the morning already.'

'Get us on the first flight to Kalgoorlie. I'll deal with the red tape and let the Kalgoorlie coppers know to be on the lookout for Snow.' Adrenalin chased away the tiredness. He drained his mug of cold coffee, shuddering as the tar-like liquid slid down his throat into his belly to rest on top of the fear and desperation to reach Lily in time.

Two hours stretched endlessly before him until finally he and Harold were seated in a turbo prop Beechcraft King Air winging their way across the desert. Mark prayed that the one-hour trip wouldn't make them too late.

Lily felt better knowing Mark was on his way, although it didn't stop her pacing the worn carpet in their room. Three hours later, she'd checked the locks and windows what felt like a hundred times as her mind worked. Serena Snow had followed them. She was on the same train, so close she could have killed them, and no one would have seen a thing. Where was she now? She knew where they were, so why hadn't she come after them yet?

For a brief moment, Lily allowed herself to regret running. She should have trusted Mark enough. If she had, they would be safe now. Instead, she'd put herself and Luke right within Serena Snow's reach. If only ...

No, no more regrets. Lily forced down the panic that constricted her throat. Let her come. Lily Bennetti was no longer a pushover, nor a trophy wife. She was damned if she'd let Serena Snow take away her second chance at freedom. Gino and Nic used fear as their weapon, and Lily had learned to manage that. Serena would come after them with her own choice of weapons and she'd manage that too.

Dawn. She had to let Dawn know they couldn't do the kitchen shift. There was no point putting themselves in Serena's path. Mark was right. It was safer to stay in their room and wait. She picked up the phone and dialled reception. After letting it ring for a while with no reply, Lily hung up. Perhaps Dawn was busy and couldn't answer. Unease trickled down her spine.

Luke paced the small room as she dialled again. 'If she's here, Mum, we're in real trouble. She'll wait for us. She knows how to play the game.'

'I know. That's why I think it's best for us not to leave the room, like Mark said,' answered Lily as she hung up. 'There's still no reply. Something's wrong, Luke. No one with a motel business lets their phone ring for that long.'

'Snow is brutal, Mum. She'll hurt anyone who gets in her way.'

'That's what worries me.' Lily tried ringing again. 'Still no response. What if she's hurt Dawn?' Ice-cold terror ripped into the pit of her stomach at the thought. How many more people would be hurt before this nightmare was over? She looked at her watch, trying to calculate how far away Mark might be. 'Luke! Come away from the window.'

'She's here. I know it. We have to help Dawn. Bring her in here with us.' Luke dropped the corner of the blind into place.

Lily's heart pounded with fear, blood roaring in her ears. 'Then we'll be in danger too.'

'I'll go. I'm the one she's looking for.' He looked at Lily, his shoulders slumped as he dragged his hoodie over his head. 'I can't let her hurt anybody else because of me.'

'No! I won't let you go.'

'I have to do this, Mum, for all of us.'

Anger, pride, guilt, regret — emotions swirled to mix with the terror in her heart. 'She'll kill you, Luke, and she won't stop there. It doesn't end with us. There'll be more victims, more children ... the next shipment of drugs. What about Marty? Will she go after him next? It won't end until she's in prison or dead.' Lily stood up from the bed and walked across to where her son stood, fists shoved into the pockets of his jeans.

'It has to end, Mum. We brought her here. We put Dawn in danger. I have to do something to stop her madness.' He turned to the door and unlocked it. 'Now *I'm* done running away.' He opened it and ran toward the reception area of the Desert Inn.

Terror ripped through Lily as he took off. With a silent prayer, she ran after him.

Mark wished Harold had hired a faster plane. Even at its maximum cruise speed of 272 knots, the Beechcraft's twin turbo propeller engines didn't move as fast as he would like. He could almost hear the clock ticking, bringing back memories of another time, another place, another hostage situation. At least he'd got his sister and niece out of that one alive. He prayed he'd have the same success with Lily and Luke.

'How much longer?' Not that he needed to ask. He'd calculated their landing within seconds of arrival time, a hundred times over, even considering the jet stream. But if he didn't talk to someone, he'd go crazy wondering what was happening in Kalgoorlie while he was helplessly suspended 25,000 feet above the never-ending, ever-changing landscape.

'We're about twenty minutes from landing,' said Jack, the pilot. 'We're waiting for the runway to clear.'

'Tell them to get a move on. This is an emergency,' Mark snapped, his patience stretched to the limit.

'Ground control is aware of that, Detective. They're doing the best they can. We've coincided with the fly-in fly-out workers. Their plane has just landed. They're getting them off as quickly as possible.' Jack turned to the controls.

'Unless you want to find yourself parachuting there, sit down and shut up. This thing might not have an eject button, but I can throw you out the door with or without a parachute,' said Harold, pulling on the tail of Mark's shirt and forcing him into a seat.

'Fuck you.'

'No, fuck you, you grumpy bastard. Put your seatbelt on.' Harold grinned.

Mark grinned although the last thing he felt like doing was smiling. The idea of losing Lily didn't even bear thinking about. What lay between them was more than a simple attraction. She'd become a part of his life so easily.

He knew when he drove up to the refuge she'd be there in the cabin he'd helped build. Every time his phone rang, he hoped ... prayed ... it was Lily's sweet voice on the other end. Every friggin' time he passed a nursery and smelled lavender, he thought of her in the garden at the refuge.

He stared out the cabin window at the earth sprawled beneath them. Dawn was breaking over Kalgoorlie casting an orange glow over the golden sands. The rambling headframes of old mine shafts passed under the belly of the plane, their sheave wheels silent against the horizon. As the plane passed over the Super Pit to make a turn, Mark watched the activity below him. Yellow trucks with wheels taller than the average person and well bodies the size of small swimming pools, wound their way up and down the narrow decline in the endless procession, some empty, some full of rocks and sand.

The minutes that ticked by felt like days and Mark wanted to scream his frustration. Every moment in the sky was time wasted, giving Serena Snow the opportunity she needed. He'd never felt this helpless, this vulnerable. His fingers clenched the edge of his seat, knuckles white and only let go when he heard the pilot announce they were coming in to land.

Out of breath, Lily chased after Luke as he pushed through the doors of the Desert Inn reception. The desk was empty, and the insistent ring of the phone echoed in the silence. Luke's sneakered feet were silent on the wooden floorboards as he checked the small office.

Lily stood behind him and peered in. There was no sign of Dawn, but the office was in turmoil. Papers littered the floor, swept off the desk. The chair lay on its side and a splash of blood stained the wall behind it. Lily moved inside, expecting to find Dawn lying dead behind the desk. She let out a shaky breath. Dawn was gone.

Luke pointed toward the kitchen door on the right. 'I'm going to check the kitchen. Stay here, Mum. Lock the door and wait for Mark,' he whispered.

'No!' Lily grabbed his arm. 'We're better off

sticking together. I can't let you go in there alone. If I lose you, Luke ...'

Luke hesitated. Lily was torn between pride and fear. She prayed they'd get out of this alive so her son could have his second chance. 'Then stay close, but when we find her, Mum, promise you'll be careful. Let me talk to her. If Gino taught me one good thing, it's how to outwit and outplay. You have to trust me.'

Lily stared at her son, wise beyond his sixteen years, far too street-savvy for her liking and cried for the boy he should be. 'I trust you.'

A touch of a smile lifted his lips. He took a deep breath and placed a shaky hand on the swing door of the kitchen. As he pushed it open, Lily caught a glimpse of Dawn seated at the table, her hair a mess and blood congealing at her temple. Behind her, with a gun in her hand, the barrel digging into the base of Dawn's neck, stood Serena Snow.

Cold horror coursed through Lily, clogging her throat and chilling her hands. Serena Snow's name suited her perfectly. With porcelain skin and ice-blonde hair, even her eyes were a frosty blue, the chill of which Lily felt on her face.

'You took your time, Liliana. Another minute and you'd have another death on your conscience.'

'Let her go, Serena. She has nothing to do with this.' Luke stepped into the kitchen.

'Ah, Luke, the snivelling little twit, the boy who was

too much of a coward to own up to being a traitor and save his own friend from dying of a drug overdose. Grow some balls on the run, did you? And you, Liliana? What are you going to do? Turn around and run away so I can shoot you in the back? Gino always said you had no backbone. But then, apparently you lacked skills in ... other areas too.'

Serena could not have chosen a better weapon against her than insecurity. The pain of her shortcomings lanced through her as Lily forced down the lump in her throat. Yes, Gino had often voiced his displeasure for her lack of initiative in the bedroom. That he'd discussed it with Serena Snow went beyond embarrassment and angered her instead. *Words, they're just words.* But they were words that brought the memories rushing back, shadows that reached out to open old wounds.

The nights he'd come home reeking of sex and perfume — she recognised it now as she caught the smell across the room — not bothering to rid himself of it before climbing into their own bed and expecting her to welcome him with open arms. Bitterness stung her throat as she remembered. No more. Gino was dead and she was damned if she'd allow this woman to continue his bullying. Her temper simmered as Serena continued with her taunts.

'I was quite happy to take care of his needs. He called you his wooden spoon, the trophy wife who wasn't such a win after all. 'Serena dug the barrel of the gun into the fleshiness of Dawn's neck and released the safety, the click loud in the tense silence.

Dawn whimpered under the pressure of Serena's hand on her shoulder and the gun at her head. Lily's heart skipped a beat as Serena's finger hovered over the trigger.

'It's me you want,' said Luke. 'Let Dawn and Mum go and take me.'

His voice was calm, but Lily saw his hands twitching at his side. She wanted to reach out to him but was too scared to in case it triggered Serena. Fear, bone-deep crawled through her blood, her heart pounded in her chest. Their time had run out. She had to do something, or this horrible, twisted woman would live, and they would die.

'What I want is to tie up the loose ends those miserable bastards left behind.' She reached around Dawn for her handbag. 'Don't worry, Dawn, I won't shoot you. Gunshots are way too messy, and bullets can be matched too easily these days. I'm going to send you on a little trip instead while Lily and Luke here watch. You'll remember this, Luke? You watched me give it to Tiny while you stood by and cried.'

The sound of the zipper grated on Lily's nerves as it amplified in the silence of the kitchen. Beside her, Luke shuddered. Lily could only imagine the horrors in his mind. Serena pulled a vial of thick, clear liquid and a syringe from her bag, and lined them up on the kitchen table.

'First, you'll feel a little burning, Dawn.' She concentrated on preparing the syringe. 'Don't try anything stupid. I really don't want to waste good drugs,' she warned as Dawn squirmed in the chair.

Lily saw the terror in the woman's eyes and felt it echoed in her stomach. Her mind worked, searching for a way that would get them all out safely. A quick glance around the room and all Lily could identify as a weapon of defence was the plastic dining chairs. Yes, there'd be knives in the kitchen drawers, but Serena stood in front of the cabinets and what use would they be when she had a gun? Could she use her little bit of self-defence training, was she strong enough? They were three to one. Surely they could overpower Serena. No, Dawn's colour wasn't healthy, and her breathing came in short gasps. Unarmed, she and Luke would be no match for Serena.

'Please don't do this, Serena,' Luke begged. 'Dawn doesn't deserve this. You're right. I'm a coward. I can't watch her die the way Tiny did.'

Serena squirted liquid from the needle then pulled back the plunger to create an airlock. 'Another waste of a life, *another* disappointing loose end, all because you couldn't keep your mouth shut, Luke. How many times did we tell you not to leave any evidence behind? But no, your mates had to try some of the merchandise and attract the cops.'

'You gave it to them!' Luke moved forward, his fear morphing into anger.

Serena shrugged. 'They didn't have to take it. They could have sold it on.'

'You bitch! You *knew* they were already addicted to the shit you and Gino made.'

'Watch your tone with me, Luke, and don't move another step or I'll shoot you without a care for the damn mess it will make.' Anger flashed in her eyes as Serena put the syringe on the table. 'Now, you know what happens when we do this, don't you? The headache, the hallucinations, the sweating, you saw it all with Tiny. Your son was there, Liliana, quaking in his hundred-dollar DCs, throwing up all over the backseat of his daddy's car. Obviously he got his courage from you.'

Rage speared through Lily, firing her blood. Had everyone thought her so weak? Was she really such a spineless, whimpering fool under Gino's control? How dare Serena suggest Luke was a coward? He was a child, forced to face things no young boy should ever have to see. Her hands itched to grab Serena around the throat and squeeze until there was no air left in her lungs. It was no longer a question of courage but of strength.

Luke stiffened and Lily felt the waves of anger heat

his body. 'Why can't you just let us go? All we want is to start over, disappear. You can go on doing what it is you do, and we'll start a new life somewhere,' he said.

'Don't be more stupid than you already are, for God's sake. Gino was right. You really are a brainless idiot. Enough chit chat,' said Serena, picking up the gun and pointing it at them. 'Come over here, Luke, and bring your mother with you. You're going to send Dawn off to Hell while I hold this gun to your mother's pretty little head. Say goodbye.'

Chapter Sixteen

Luke picked up the syringe filled with a deadly cocktail of hallucinogens and methamphetamines.

'Tell your mother what happens when it goes into your system. What too much too fast can do in your bloodstream,' Serena taunted as she pulled Lily forward by the arm, her fingers digging cruelly into the flesh and jamming the gun against her temple.

Luke remained silent, pushing back his hoodie.

'*Tell* her!'

He flinched at the harshness of Serena's voice.

'Enough!' cried Lily. 'Leave him alone! We know what it does, Serena! It kills people. *You* kill people.'

'I wasn't talking to you, Liliana. Did you want some, Luke? You know you do. Remember what it's like as it pulses through your blood? That rush of adrenalin. The strength you feel, the confidence. You can conquer *everything*, you're capable of *anything* — even killing your own mother.'

'Stop!' Luke shouted.

'Go on, Luke, no point wasting time. No one is coming to rescue you this time. I want your mother to see how she's going to die, struggling against it, hallucinating, screaming with pain from the fire in her veins.'

The twisted sound of Serena's laugh raised the hair on Lily's arms. Her hopes that Mark would come in time faded fast as she faced reality. They were on their own. There would be no dramatic rescue. It was kill or be killed. The realisation struck deep that it would make them no better than Gino. They'd run out of choices, out of time. Whatever Luke had planned was no match for Serena. He was just a boy. Desperate to avoid the horror of watching Dawn die, Lily used the only weapon she had.

'You'd do this to a *boy*? Force a *child* to murder his mother and an innocent woman? You're a mother too, Serena. Eighteen years ago, you abandoned your baby — your son — in a hospital in Port Hedland.'

Serena's eyes flickered. 'What the hell are you talking about? You're wrong.'

'Nic Albero was his father.'

Serena's pale, translucent skin flushed an angry red. 'Bullshit! Luke! Give the old woman her fucking shot *now.*' She grabbed Lily around the neck, the gun pressing painfully against her skull.

Lily choked and fought against Serena's grip, desperation overriding fear as she clawed at the woman's arms. 'Let her go, Serena! You can kill us, but the truth will still be out there. Mark Johnson will still be on your tail.' She struggled to swallow the panic, the dread, the fading hope that just beyond the door, Mark waited for the right moment to smash it down.

'Your time is running out. Whatever bullshit tale you're spinning, spit it out.' Serena's grip tightened. 'I had a baby, yes. He was premature and they said he wouldn't live.'

'He lived until *you* killed him. Tiny Watts was the baby you abandoned in Port Hedland. You murdered your own son.'

Mark had the door of the Beechcraft ready to lower as it taxied to a stop on the runway at Kalgoorlie airport. He sprinted as fast as the narrow steps would allow and headed toward the police car they'd radioed ahead for. Fear had burned a hole in his stomach already and dread added to the pain.

'Fill me in,' he said, slamming the car door behind him.

'I have an emergency response team armed and

ready to go at your word. We checked the Desert Inn about an hour ago and everything was normal. There's no sign of Snow. I've had the boys on the lookout since your alert a couple of hours ago. I checked with Dawn at the Desert Inn at 4:00 a.m. Lily and Luke were safely in their room.' Detective Inspector Ned Howes turned the key in the ignition and started the car as soon as Harold opened the rear door. 'Let's go.'

'Did you leave a man at the motel?' Mark asked.

'No, it was all clear as I said. I sent them out to check the area within a 5km radius, hoping we'd spot her before she got there,' Ned responded. 'I tell you, I'll be a happy man if I can throw that bitch's arse in prison. I've been trying to crack that syndicate for years.' He paused as he turned the car toward town. 'This week alone we intercepted three drug shipments heading north. The highway is a hot spot for trafficking.'

The knot of fear in Mark's stomach tightened. 'You'll have to stand in line, mate. I need to have a little chat with her first. I've got enough to charge her with, but God help her if she's hurt Lily or Luke — or anyone else. Can you drive a little faster?'

Ned floored the accelerator pedal and the V8 engine roared as the pursuit car surged forward. 'This could bring down one of the biggest syndicates world-wide, equating to millions of dollars-worth of meth. It would certainly make my job easier and my town a whole lot nicer. I could go back to handing out parking tickets for a while.'

Mark bristled. This was more than a drug bust. 'Let's not forget the lives at stake here.' He felt Harold's warning hand on his shoulder and shook it off irritably.

Ned looked across at him. 'I understand that. We've lost enough lives in this town to the trade. I don't need to add to the body count.' He pulled up outside the Desert Inn. 'That's weird. Dawn should be in the kitchen prepping for breakfast but the lights in there are still off.' He pointed to the building that ran at an angle to the motel. The windows under the overhanging roof were dark against the clay-coloured wall.

Mark and Harold didn't hesitate.

Serena Snow's roar of outrage sliced through the tension in the room. 'You're a lying bitch! Stop stalling for time!' She grabbed Lily's hair and forced her head back, pressing the gun into the soft flesh under her chin. 'Tiny Watts was a street kid. My baby died. They said he wouldn't live more than twenty-four hours.'

Lily ignored the pain that ripped through her skull. 'You're wrong. He lived until he was eighteen, moving between foster families or living on the streets. I've seen his birth certificate. He was born July 25th at the public hospital in Port Hedland. You abandoned him and left him to the mercy of the foster system without looking back. Serena Snow is your maiden name. Your married name is Serena Maria Watts. I found your marriage certificate in with Tiny's birth certificate. You left your whole *life* at the hospital and walked away. Did you ever — just once — wonder what had happened to your baby, Serena?'

'Shut up! You know *nothing* of life on the streets, you pampered bitch. Struggling to make a buck so you can eat. Prostituting yourself to pricks like Nic Albero so you can get your hands on the stuff that makes you forget how you got there,' Serena yelled as she pulled a rubber tube from her pocket and threw it at Luke. 'Get the fucking job done! You're next.'

'I won't let you murder my son like you murdered yours!'

Lily slammed her elbow into Serena's stomach, satisfaction warming her blood as the impact sent her stumbling backwards. A chair toppled over with a crash as Serena fell against it. She lost her footing and landed hard on her backside, the gun spinning away.

Lily scrambled to her feet, picked up the gun and aimed it squarely at Serena. Luke wasted no time either. He grabbed Serena in a neck hold and pressed the needle of the syringe against her neck. 'How does that feel, huh? All I have to do is jab it in and press the plunger, and you'll die just like Tiny did.' She tried to dislodge him, but he clung to her throat, squeezing hard against her wind pipe.

'Luke, no! It's not worth it. *She's* not worth going to prison for. Get that syringe away from her neck. Don't do it, baby,' Lily pleaded. *Déjà vu* darkened her world once more.

The door to the kitchen crashed open and feet pounded across the tiles. Luke dropped the syringe and stood with his hands in the air. Lily kept the gun aimed squarely on Serena, her finger trembling on the trigger, her thumb ready to cock the shot. It would be so easy, she thought, so easy to finish it. A familiar warm hand covered hers and pushed it downwards gently to lower the gun.

'Give me that, love. It's okay now. Harold's got her covered.' Mark's voice washed over her, warm and soothing.

She hesitated. The urge to kill the woman who'd destroyed their lives was strong. They'd lost so much because of her. Mark's body was warm against her back as he moved to put an arm around her waist and remove the gun from her hand with the other. She let him take it.

He turned her in his arms and held her tightly against his chest, stroking her hair with a soothing touch. She felt him press a kiss on top of her head and heard the rumble of his voice against her ear. 'Are you okay, Luke?'

'Yeah, but Dawn needs help. Serena whacked her a mean shot against the head.'

'I've taken care of it,' said Harold. 'The ambulance will be here in a minute or two. The locals are taking Snow away and locking her up for us. Want to come with me, son?' he said to Luke. 'I think Detective Johnson here has a few questions for your mum and I know I want to ask you a few too.'

Luke hesitated and Lily lifted her head from the warm comfort of Mark's chest. 'It's okay, Luke, go. It's over, baby, it's over.'

'Will you be okay, Mum?'

Lily smiled. 'We'll be okay, Luke.'

He nodded and followed Harold out the room. Lily looked up into Mark's eyes. He smiled at her, and she thought she'd never seen such a beautiful sight. Her heart pounded at the promise in his eyes. As the room emptied out around them, he held her and simply looked.

'Thank you,' she said to him as the paramedics carried Dawn out on a stretcher, her head bandaged and the painkillers kicking in.

'I thought I was too late,' he said, trailing his finger over her cheek. He tucked her hair behind her ear. 'I'm in love with you, Lily.'

Lily pressed her cheek into his palm, closed her eyes and allowed herself a moment to dream. 'It's not over yet, Mark', she whispered.

'No, but when it is, I will still love you.'

He lowered his head and touched his lips to hers. She returned his kiss, glorying in the warm tenderness, her imagination running wild with thoughts of where that kiss might lead one day. She lifted her hand to his head to bring him closer still, standing on tip toe to enjoy the feel of his body against hers and the euphoria of being alive as her blood sang through her veins.

Harold cleared his throat in the doorway. 'We have a plane to catch. Olive is going to be heartbroken.'

Mark lifted his head and smiled at Lily. 'Let's go home.'

Chapter Seventeen

An hour later the plane was fuelled up and ready to go. They'd stopped at the hospital to check on Dawn with a promise to come back for a less eventful visit.

Now, settled into the seat of the plane, Lily leaned back to do up her seatbelt. She looked up to find Mark's face so close to hers, she could see the day's growth of beard darkening his jawline and the deep lines of a frown on his face. She lifted her hand and placed her palm against the warmth of his face, stroked her thumb over the groove near the curve of his lips. He stilled and turned stormy grey eyes to hers. In them she saw a promise that made her blood sing with hope.

'Thank you,' whispered Lily as she leaned forward a little and placed a soft kiss a little to the left of his lips, inhaling the warm scent of him. She imagined waking up in his arms, the firm heat of his body against hers, the feel of his skin under her touch and the pleasure she knew would follow. This was true love. Not the idea of love she'd had when she met Gino but a love that would survive the toughest challenges and bring them closer instead of driving them apart.

Mark looked at her a moment longer, heat flaring in his eyes. 'You're welcome.'

If they were alone, she would crawl into his lap and take advantage of the invitation in his eyes. She looked up to where Luke sat in the co-pilot's seat like he was born to be there, bombarding Harold and Jack with questions as they went through the final flight checks. Harold didn't seem to mind the teen's questions, so she settled down to enjoy the flight.

She turned her head to look at Mark. He sat with his head resting against the seatback. Tired lines etched his mouth. She reached up to touch them again. He turned and pressed his lips against her fingers. She left them there and enjoyed the sensation of them against her skin.

He took her hand in his and threaded his fingers with hers. There was no need for words. His eyes held all the unspoken promise she needed. Her heart skipped a beat as her mind ran riot with images of twisted sheets and satisfied sighs. In just one look, there was the promise of happiness she'd never imagined having the opportunity to experience. With a sigh, she rested her head against the seat and closed her eyes. The plane taxied down the runway and she said goodbye to a past best forgotten.

~

'Lily.'

Warm fingers stroked her cheek. She turned into the warmth and comfort of a broad, muscular shoulder, felt the tickle of Mark's beard at her temple and sighed.

'Lily, honey,' Mark whispered, 'we're coming in to land.'

Lily groaned and shifted. The ache of the muscles in her shoulders registered through the cloudiness of sleep. She lifted her head and moved to sit upright in her seat, a little stiff from sleeping in the awkward position. Her hand was still held tightly in Mark's. She smiled.

'I'd love to take you home to clean up, but we have to check in at the station with Luke first.'

Mark's words cleared the remnants of sleep from her mind and replaced it with heaviness in her heart. 'Is he under arrest for breaking his bail conditions?'

'No, love, we need to fill in some paperwork to cover the delay in his checking in. We also need to take your statements on what happened in Kalgoorlie. I'd delay it if I could, but Serena will be transported back here tomorrow, and I want all the red tape tied up nice and tight when she arrives.'

Lily nodded. 'I understand. Is it really over, Mark?'

The wheels of the Beechcraft touched down on the runway at Jandakot airport with a squeal and a bump. Up in the co-pilot's seat, Luke gave a whoop and high-fived Harold.

'Almost.' Mark let go of her hand, leaned over and unclipped her seat belt as they taxied to a stop. 'Giles Pritchard has a date set for Luke's court case. Given the new evidence and what happened today with Serena Snow, the court has brought his case forward.'

Lily sighed. Soon they'd know the outcome of the case and what their future held. 'When?'

'In three weeks. We'll have the investigation wrapped up and the evidence ready to go.' He helped her up out of the seat. 'Not long now and you and Luke can start again. I want you to know I'll be there waiting, Lily.'

In the close confines of the cabin, Lily absorbed the heat and strength that emanated from him. She closed her eyes for a moment and inhaled the heady combination. When she opened them again, he stood close and placed an arm around her shoulders, gently nudging her out into the aisle between the seats.

They exited the plane in silence, each with their own thoughts on what starting over might mean.

'Please stand.' The bailiff's voice echoed through the almost empty courtroom.

Lily squeezed Luke's hand and for once, he didn't pull away. She sat on the hard wooden bench as he stepped forward to take his place next to his lawyer. His physical scars had healed during the seemingly endless investigation into Gino's death, but the emotional scars would take far longer. They'd spent the last three weeks recovering from their ordeal with Serena Snow, making endless statements, answering questions and giving evidence in her preliminary hearing.

Luke's trial had taken its toll on both of them. Their future now rested with the judge's decision. Lily glanced around the courtroom. There were only a few people in the room. Mark and Harold sat to her right in the gallery behind the dock where Luke and Giles Pritchard waited for the verdict. To her left, TJ, Scott and Marty waited just as impatiently. Their love and support had gone a long way in helping her and Luke heal, but it wouldn't be over until Luke's sentence was delivered. As the judge entered the courtroom, Lily turned to face her, held her breath and prayed.

Judge Julia Carmody sat and arranged her robes around her. 'Please, be seated.' Her stern voice called for silence as chairs shuffled on the wooden floorboards. She leaned back and looked directly at Luke. 'Mr Bennetti, I do not condone murder under any circumstances.'

A chill ran up Lily's spine. *Oh God.*

'However,' the judge continued, 'I don't believe what you did was pre-meditated murder and I do believe you acted — not only in self-defence — but to protect your mother. I also don't believe it was proved sufficiently that you pulled that trigger. The way I see it, it was a tragic accident brought on by extenuating circumstances.' She leaned forward and clasped her hands together, her eyes not leaving Luke's. 'Therefore, according to Section 418 of the Crimes Act 1900, on the charge of Involuntary Manslaughter, I find you ... not guilty.'

Lily released the breath she was holding and buried her face in her hands. Relief flooded through her. *Thank God!*

'Thank you, Ma'am,' said Luke.

'Don't thank me, son. It's not over yet. There's still the little matter of why you had the gun and why you were pointing it at your father,' Judge Carmody said with a wave of her hand.

Lily's hands and legs shook, fear settled in the pit of her stomach at the verdict the judge would deliver. In the dock in front of her, Luke trembled, his knuckles white in the fists he held at his side.

'It would be remiss of me to let you go unpunished for taking another person's life, whether it was an accident or in self-defence. From the evidence presented, I am ruling that the defendant killed the deceased in self-defence. On the charge of being in under-age possession and discharging a firearm without a license, I find you guilty. A charge that carries a five-year minimum sentence, I might remind you.' She paused to let the severity of the charges sink in. 'However, due to the extenuating circumstances, I am sentencing you to four years of Community Service, considering the time you have already spent enrolled in the Apprenticeship Rehabilitation program run by Scott and Tiffany Devin at their dealership, M&M Motors. You will remain in the program for the full course of the apprenticeship, which is four years and in that time, remain in residence at the centre under the guardianship of the Devins. During that time, any misconduct will find you back in this court and I'll have you remanded in juvenile custody. Understood?'

Lily felt the warmth of Mark's hand on hers, squeezing lightly. She looked up to meet the smile in his eyes and released a breath of relief at the sentence Luke received. God knows, they'd been punished enough. Second chances didn't always come that easy and she prayed her son would make the best of the reprieve he'd been granted.

'Yes, Judge Carmody.' Luke shuffled his feet but kept eye contact with the stern judge.

She nodded. 'The reports I received from the Devins paint a glowing picture of your behaviour, maturity and work ethic. I expect that to continue. You may leave with the Devins now, Mr Bennetti. Don't let me see you in my courtroom again. I expect a full quarterly behaviour report from the rehabilitation centre until the end of the sentence.'

'Thank you, Ma'am.'

As the judge left the courtroom, Luke turned and wrapped his mother in a hug. Almost a head shorter than him, Lily placed her arms around his skinny waist and hugged him, despite the wooden barrier between them.

Hugs, handshakes and backslaps followed as they took a moment to enjoy the victory. TJ threw her arms around Lily and hugged her hard.

'The cabin is your home for as long as you want it, Lily. Even though we're Luke's legal guardians, he still needs his mum. We're all about encouraging a family environment. And your job is waiting for you at M&M. I'll be glad to have you there. I'm really impressed at the progress you've made already.'

'Thank you,' said Lily, hugging her. 'I will pay back the money I took too. I can't wait to get into the garden ... if that's okay with you?'

TJ stepped back, keeping a hold on Lily's hands. 'I was hoping you'd say that! I think Bill is missing you. He's driving Rose crazy asking when you'll be home.'

Lily smiled, and for the first time since she'd met and married Gino Bennetti, she smiled a real smile. One that came from deep within her, radiated through her and lit up her eyes as laughter lines crinkled at the corners. 'It's good to be home,' she said.

With one last squeeze, TJ moved on to Luke. As Lily watched the group enfold Luke in a hug, she felt the warmth of a hard male body at her back. She turned to stand close to Mark, looking up into his face. Tension zinged between them as they stood, an invisible cord tugging them closer.

'I can't thank you enough for believing in us, for setting us free,' she said.

He opened his mouth as if to say something but closed it again. Instead, he let his hand drift up to her face and stroked his fingers over the scar on her cheek. Gently, he tucked a strand of her hair behind her ear. Lily placed her hand over his, drawing it down to entwine their fingers. He closed his eyes as he placed a kiss in the valley between their fingers.

'To new beginnings.'

'To new beginnings,' she echoed, knowing there was still one matter left to resolve before they could move on.

Chapter Eighteen

The day of Gino Bennetti's cremation was damp and gloomy. Hell and Heaven prepared for him with thunder and lightning, thought Lily. In the chapel, the small group she now regarded as her family, sat in silence as the celebrant read the committal.

With Luke at her side, they paused at the closed coffin and said goodbye to the man who'd caused them immeasurable pain. Lily cried, not for the man she'd lost but for the man he could have been. Luke stood silent, tearless, and expressionless. Lily understood his difficulty to mourn a man who sacrificed lives for the sake of money.

She turned to look up at Mark as he stepped up behind them and placed a comforting arm around their shoulders. After a moment, he led them out the chapel as the sun broke through the gloom.

'Ready?' he asked.

Lily nodded. 'Let's go home.'

He held onto Lily's hand and kept an arm around Luke's shoulders as he led them to the car. A comfortable silence stretched between them as they drove up the hill to the centre where Rose waited with freshly baked muffins and brewed coffee.

In the kitchen, Luke helped himself to two muffins and a mug of hot chocolate. 'I'll be at the creek with Sarge, Mum. Will you tell Marty where I am?'

'Sure. You okay, Luke?' Lily rubbed a hand down his skinny arm.

'Yeah, I'm okay.' A smile twitched at his lips and Lily thought it was the most beautiful thing she'd seen in weeks.

'Good,' she replied with a smile of her own. She watched him call to Sarge and make his way out the door.

'Need some company, son?' she heard Bill call out as Luke passed by the lounge where he watched a football match while he dozed.

'Sure,' came Luke's response.

'I'll keep an eye on him from the veranda,' said Mark.

'Thanks. I'll bring your coffee out to you.' Lily smiled up at him, happiness spreading through her.

'Welcome home,' Rose said, enveloping her in a warm hug. 'I'm so glad it's over, honey. Now you can get your life together again. We wanted you to know that you're welcome to stay as long as you need to. You're part of our family now. Now run along outside and snuggle up to that delicious hero we have sitting outside waiting for his coffee. I want to get the last batch of muffins into the oven before TJ and Scott get home with Marty. I swear that boy eats like a horse!'

'Please tell me you're not matchmaking, Rose?'

Rose looked at her, a cheeky grin on her lips. 'Oh honey, I don't think I have to. Our detective's eyes follow you everywhere. Off you go now ... and Lily?'

'Yes, Rose?'

'Be happy. There's a man out there who loves you and wants to take care of you the way you deserve to be cared for, child.'

Lily smiled. 'We'll see.'

Outside on the veranda, Lily handed Mark a mug of steaming coffee and sat on the couch beside him. She scooted into the corner, drew her legs up and tucked them in under her bum.

'I can't believe it's finally over. Thank you.'

Mark sipped at the coffee, the best he'd had in days. Courtroom coffee was worse than police department coffee. He bent forward and placed the mug on the table before leaning back on the couch. He turned his head to look at her ... his tired, bedraggled angel. She'd lost weight over the weeks since Gino's death, something he planned on spending the rest of his life remedying. The trial had been hard on all of them, dredging up memories no-one wanted or needed brought to the surface, aired with the help of the media.

He leaned forward again to take her mug and placed it on the table next to his. With a tug on her hands, he drew her to him, pleased when she didn't resist. She nestled into the comfort of his arms, her head on the warmth of his chest, his heart beating a rapid tattoo against her ear. His stomach tightened as her hand stroked across his chest and down his side to rest on his hip.

Lily looked up at him and smiled. He ran a finger across the fading scar on her cheek, tipped her chin up further. 'No-one will ever hurt you or Luke again. I promise. Not on my watch.'

'Does that mean you'll be hanging around, Detective?'

'Would you like me to?' His gaze roamed her face, coming to rest on her lips ... such kissable lips.

'I think so.'

'You *think* so? Let me convince you.' His voice was a whisper as he pressed his lips to hers, a light touch that coaxed her closer. The warmth of his hand travelled over her hip and under her bottom as he hitched her onto his lap. 'I love you, Lily, your strength, your courage, your smile. I want to see more of that smile. I want to wake up next to you with your perfume on my pillows and the warmth of you in my arms. Is that okay?'

Lily nodded, her hand creeping up his chest, across his collar bone and over the curve of his bicep. 'I've wanted to do that for a while now,' she whispered, as she trailed her hand up around his neck. 'I think I'm in love with you too.'

She pulled his head down and Mark followed her lead as she tested his lips with hers. He stroked the curve of her bottom through the material of her skirt, and she inched closer. Lily deepened the kiss with a sigh. He shifted beneath the power of it as his body responded.

'If you keep that up, Miss Lily, I'm not going to be able to think straight in a minute,' he said, a little breathlessly as he broke away while he still could.

She smiled, that gentle, impish tug of the lips, her eyes twinkling with mischief. *God*, he loved seeing his Lily like this. She shifted against him, and he groaned, cupping her bottom to pull her closer so she could feel his need. He ran a hand over the silky skin of her legs, up under the skirt and over her thigh.

'Am I rushing you, Lily? Tell me if I am. It's so soon after —'

'No. You're not rushing me,' she said, tracing his lips with her forefinger. 'I didn't bury my husband today. I buried a stranger, a criminal, a bully. Any love I had for Gino died long before he did. What I feel for you is completely different. You make me feel loved, safe, cared for.'

'All the things I want for you.'

'Then let's stop thinking too much,' she said, echoing his own words to her.

With a gentle sigh, she placed her lips against his, tasted his mouth, and coaxed him with the velvet of her tongue, while her hands worked across his shoulders, down his arms, onto his waist.

Drowning in the smell and taste of her, he barely registered the roar of an engine in the drive, doors slamming and Marty's excitement as he ran off to the creek, calling for Luke and Sarge. Every inch of her body touched him, cried out for more. Heat surged through him as he lifted her away a little and dragged his lips from hers.

'This may have to wait until later, love. We have company. *Jesus*, Lily!'

Her chuckle against his neck was almost his undoing as he surged under her, pressing into the palm of her hand when she trailed a hand over the front of his jeans. She pressed a kiss into the V of his neck above his shirt. He cupped her face with his hand as she stretched against him.

'Hold that thought,' she whispered.

'Oh, I will, Lily, and later, I'll love you as you deserve to be loved.' He lifted her gently off his lap, keeping her close to him in the crook of his arm.

'I'll hold you to that promise ... forever,' she whispered as Scott and TJ mounted the stairs to the veranda.

Under the star-dappled sky in Tiny's Garden, they drank a toast to him and barbequed his favourite Angus Beef burgers. By the light from the half-built gazebo, Luke and Marty made a start on the mural, their graffiti no longer dark or filled with secret codes and messages. Instead, they drew a promise of life and the freedom they could enjoy now Snow and Albero were locked away, both serving life sentences for manslaughter.

TJ yawned and stretched, bumping her shoulder against Scott's. 'That's me done. I'm knackered. Let's go to bed, honey.'

Scott chuckled. 'Best invitation I've had all day.' He stood, scooped her up, tossed her over his shoulder in a fireman's lift and jogged off down to the house, calling out, 'Night all,' over TJ's squeals.

Lily's laughter faded as Mark reached for her hand and whispered, 'What say we leave the boys to their swags and the mercy of the mosquitoes?' His gaze burned on hers, filled with promise.

Lily shivered as she nodded. He hoped it was not with fear but expectation. Mark stood and drew her to his side, warming her cold hand with his. He squeezed her fingers reassuringly. His heart hammered in his chest now as desire swirled through him. Finally, he thought, this was his chance to show Lily what it was like to truly love and be loved.

'Stay, Sarge,' Mark called to the Rottweiler. The need for a guard dog might be over but he figured Sarge would be devastated to miss the excitement of a camp out under the stars with the boys. 'Night, guys.'

'Night,' Luke and Marty chorused, not looking up from their artwork.

'Ready?' Gently, he smoothed the frown from Lily's brow with a light touch. If she wasn't, he'd go home and wait until she was, but he hoped to God she wouldn't send him away tonight. If all he did was hold her close as she slept, he'd be happy with that.

The flicker of a smile crossed her lips as she turned to make her way down the hill toward her cabin, tugging him behind her. She pushed open the door and led him inside, stopping as he closed it firmly and turned the key in the lock. The sound echoed between them as Lily left her past behind and turned to her future. She stepped into the circle of Mark's arms and raised her face to his.

'I'm ready.'

He released a nervous breath on a chuckle and hugged her close for a brief moment. Then his lips brushed across hers, lightly testing her response.

Lily felt that sweep of his kiss all the way to her toes as she sighed, parting her lips to invite him in. His big, comforting hands cupped her face, thumbs stroking her cheekbones reassuringly to match the rhythm of his searching mouth ... a rhythm she answered with her own promise.

Her hands found his firm hips and travelled up under his shirt to touch the warm, smooth contours of his back, drawing him closer until their bodies aligned and she felt the press of him against her. Dizzying need scrambled her thoughts and tugged at her muscles as she pictured him naked, a vision she knew would be real before long. Lingering doubts forced their way to the forefront of her mind, momentarily overriding the passion. Lily drew back a little and he lifted his head. She missed the warm promise of his lips immediately.

'Okay?' he whispered.

'I'm a little scared.' She raised her eyes to his. 'What if ... Gino said ...'

Mark dropped his hands from her face, stroked a gentle path down her arms and cupped her hands in his. 'What did Gino say?'

'That ... that I suck at sex.' Torn between desire and insecurity, Lily dropped her gaze to their joined hands.

'Lily, look at me,' Mark said, his tone gentle and patient.

She did, knowing she wore her heart in her eyes. There was nothing she wanted more than to love this man who made her feel alive again, but still her insecurities stood in the path of bliss.

'No one sucks at sex. Not if you love someone with your heart and soul ... like I love you. Teach me, Lily. Show me how to love you. There is no right or wrong way, only our way.' He lifted her hands to his chest, anchored them between their bodies as he cupped her hips and drew her closer.

Her touch hesitant, Lily ran her hands across the width of his chest, up his shoulders and into the hair that skimmed his nape. She stood on tiptoes to draw his head down and press her lips to his, testing his response. With each encouraging whisper from Mark, Lily grew bolder with her touch until the passion between them demanded the barrier of clothing be gone.

Sweeping her into his arms, Mark carried Lily into the bedroom, her lips pressed to the curve of his shoulder. She protested as he broke the contact to lay her down across the covers.

With a tenderness she'd never experienced before, Mark removed her clothes, taking his time to caress every inch of exposed skin until Lily thought she'd die from the sensations that flooded through her. Every nerve end sparked at the light graze of his touch. Muscles once unaffected, contracted with each feather-light kiss he dropped on her skin. As the final barrier fell away, leaving her naked and exposed to his gaze, he murmured, 'I love you, my beautiful Lily. No-one will ever make you feel unwanted or unloved again.'

Her body languid with desire, her mind floating in

sensation, Lily reached for Mark's shirt. He obliged by lifting his arms, allowing her to draw it over his head and toss it aside. The vision she'd had earlier of him naked hadn't prepared her for the real thing. Her gaze wandered across the expanse of his chest as her fingers traced the scars of his trade. Each one told a story of what had made him the man he was — a strong, hard and merciless cop, yet a gentle, caring, dependable lover when needed ... and oh boy, did Lily need him. She reached for his belt and removed the final hurdle that kept them apart, taking a moment to admire him in all his unclothed glory.

The mattress dipped under his weight and soon she felt the slide of his skin on hers, the touch of his lips caressing parts of her body never before explored with such devotion. With each touch, each kiss, her confidence grew until the room was filled with breathless sighs, then silence except for the rhythm of love and murmured adoration.

Later, as Lily lay sprawled across Mark's warm body, well and truly satisfied, she knew there was no need for words to tell him how much she loved him. She'd shown him with every inch of her soul — and now, with his strong arms securely around her, the slowing rise and fall of his chest against her breasts, she slept secure in the knowledge she'd found love.

Dear Reader, This book has been written and edited using Australian / UK English grammar and punctuation conventions because the story is set in Australia. For more information on the differences between UK and US language and punctuation, please consider reading this article: https://tinyurl.com/56tkbh6a

If you enjoyed this book, please consider leaving a review on BookBub, Goodreads or the platform you purchased it from. If you would prefer to email me, please visit the contact page on my website at https://juanitakees.com/contact/. I do love to hear from readers and welcome your feedback.

Kind regards

Juanita Kees

Exposed, Tagged and Silenced (Unfinished Business series) can be purchased from your favourite bookseller. If they don't have it, ask them or your local library to order it in for you.

Other Books by Juanita Kees

Wongan Creek Series

Whispers

Secrets

Shadows

Unfinished Business

Exposed

Tagged

Silenced

Bindarra Creek

Home to Bindarra Creek

Promise Me Forever

The Calhouns of Montana

Montana Baby

Montana Daughter

Montana Son

Contemporary Romance

Finish Line

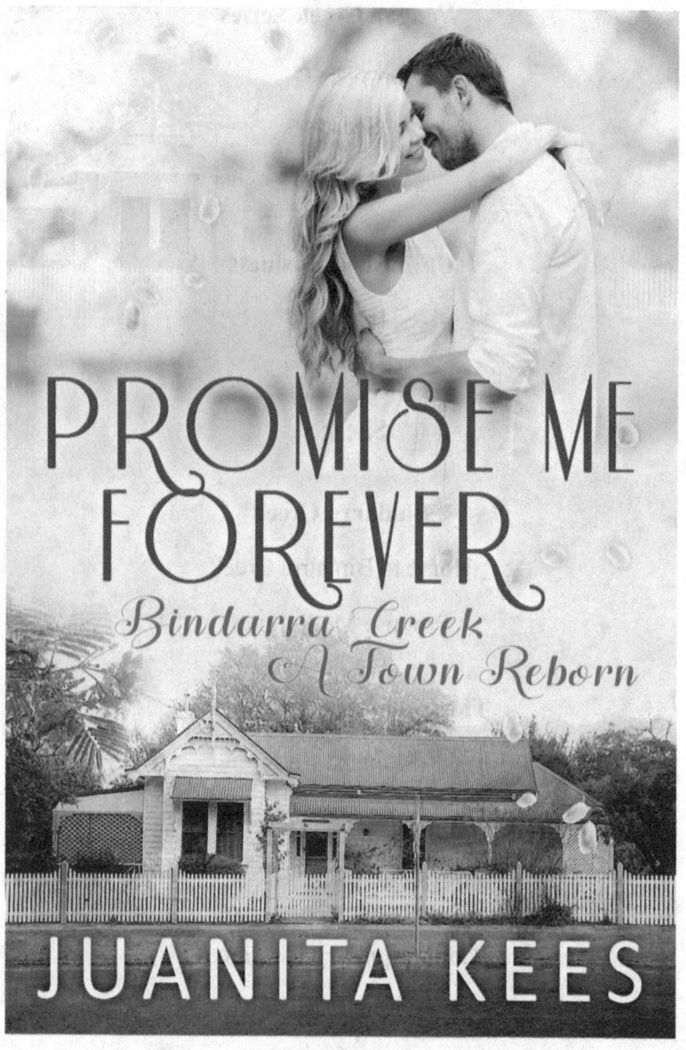

*PROMISE ME FOREVER (Bindarra Creek Series) - By
Juanita Kees*

9 780645 631944